What the critics are saying:

"Don't miss an excellent, one-of-a-kind book by Shiloh Walker. If you thought TOUCH OF GYPSY FIRE was her best novel yet, the tales in this collection will surely go down as her greatest and most memorable short stories (at least so far)." - *Enya Adrian, Romance Reviews Today*

"MYTHE & MAGICK is a one-author anthology featuring three feisty heroines and the men who need them. All of the stories feature some paranormal aspect, from psychic powers to real magick, and all three are quick, pleasure-filled reads...Walker outdoes herself in this heated, magical collection that celebrates both the mystery of magic and the ultimate strength of woman herself." - *Ann Leveille, Sensual Romance Reviews*

"Shiloh Walker takes us to the realms of Mythe & Magick in her newest anthology...All three stories teach the reader that finding love will help make your dreams come true. Once you find that special person, you'll truly find yourself and your place in the world." - *Jenni, A Romance Review*

"This magical, mythical realm will not disappoint paranormal lovers..." - *Angel Brewer, The Romance Studio*

MYTHE & MAGICK

By Shiloh Walker

MYTHE & MAGICK
An Ellora's Cave Publication, December 2004

Ellora's Cave Publishing, Inc.
PO Box 787
Hudson, OH 44236-0787

ISBN #1-4199-5115-7

ISBN MS Reader (LIT) ISBN # 1-84360-859-6
Other available formats (no ISBNs are assigned):
Adobe (PDF), Rocketbook (RB), Mobipocket (PRC) & HTML

Edited by *Pamela Campbell*
Cover art by *Syneca*

Warning:

The following material contains graphic sexual content meant for mature readers. *MYTHE & MAGIC* has been rated E–rotic by a minimum of three independent reviewers.

Ellora's Cave Publishing offers three levels of Romantica™ reading entertainment: S (S-ensuous), E (E-rotic), and X (X-treme).

S-*ensuous* love scenes are explicit and leave nothing to the imagination.

E-*rotic* love scenes are explicit, leave nothing to the imagination, and are high in volume per the overall word count. In addition, some E-rated titles might contain fantasy material that some readers find objectionable, such as bondage, submission, same sex encounters, forced seductions, etc. E-rated titles are the most graphic titles we carry; it is common, for instance, for an author to use words such as "fucking", "cock", "pussy", etc., within their work of literature.

X-*treme* titles differ from E-rated titles only in plot premise and storyline execution. Unlike E-rated titles, stories designated with the letter X tend to contain controversial subject matter not for the faint of heart.

MYTHE & MAGICK

Dedication

To my editor Pam, the Wondrous One.

*To my kids Cam and Jess — my world revolves around you
two. I love you both.*

And to my husband Jerry. My real life fantasy… I love you.

AVALON

Chapter One
June 1999

If he was honest, it was that cool, icy composure that had first attracted him. She was like a rose encased in ice, and he was drawn to bring her out. And God help him if any of their co-workers had any inkling just how poetic his thoughts became when Seth thought of Erin.

Her hair fell halfway down her back in razor-straight silky tresses of pale, pale blonde, brows just slightly darker arching over pale, ice-blue eyes. Her skin was ivory and peaches and as soft as satin.

And the taste of her…

Man, the taste of her was pure sex. Again, she brought peaches to mind, hot juicy, ripe peaches just plucked from the tree. She was addictive.

Erin Sinclair was every man's dream. She offered no promises, accepted none, asked for none. She didn't steal the covers at night and didn't presume that simply spending the night meant a wedding ring. In bed, she was hot and wild and everything Seth could hope for.

Yep, Erin Sinclair was every man's dream.

Every man but Seth Porter.

Because she was every bit as distant as the stars.

And he was head-over-heels in love with her. Seth wanted nothing more than to promise her the moon, and have her make the same promise back to him.

Currently, the object of his brooding thoughts sat some fifteen feet away, calmly working on a report in the midst of the chaos of the bullpen. All around, voices were raised, the voices of pleading suspects, weeping mothers, raging fathers, harassed overworked public defenders, and under it all, the voices of the detectives that worked the 53rd precinct of Avalon Police Department.

Avalon. Man, what a joke. This city was as far from perfect as it could possibly be. Oh, it had a well-to-do area where the doctors and lawyers drove their Mercedes with lily-white, smooth hands, where the lawns were manicured and green and lush.

But that area was small, isolated, an island surrounded by crime, corruption, and chaos. The rest of Avalon sat so far apart that they may as well have been in different countries, never mind the fact that they shared the same area code.

Seth Porter was from that part of Avalon, where prostitutes, druggies, and derelicts ran wild. Seth was a bastard, plain and simple, and had no qualms about admitting it. His father, most likely Italian, had taken what he wanted from his momma while she worked as a cocktail waitress and part-time stripper at a sleazy Avalon night spot called The Lady of Avalon. If he had promised her the world and a diamond ring and a ticket out of this hellhole, Anita Porter had never mentioned it to Seth.

Instead she accepted the fact that she had been naïve and started working double shifts, saving as much money as she could before she started to show and got booted out on her fanny.

After that, she had applied for a job at the precinct and for some odd, completely obscure reason, had landed it, and worked there to this day. She'd worked her way from the janitorial staff up to secretary, did a brief spot as dispatcher, and then worked her way into the archives. Anita ran her own little kingdom in the precinct with an iron fist and even the most hardened, jaded detective knew better than take a file from her precious room without signing it out.

And heaven help him if he kept it any longer than she felt was necessary.

Seth threw his pen down on the table and shoved the report away. Glancing at the clock, he scowled, realizing just how late it was.

Erin. He could tune out everything in the bullpen, the voices of the damned, the smell of unwashed bodies and tobacco and stale alcohol, the clacking of typewriters and the hum of computers and modems.

But he could not, for the life of him, block Erin Sinclair from his mind.

Erin truly was a lady of Avalon, the daughter of one of the well-respected, well-to-do members of the inner set. Mr. Eric Sinclair had run the top accounting firm in the city, and had his hand in some of the finer real estate pieces in several of the surrounding cities. He had been upright, he had been honest, and he was a decent enough person, even if he did have a bit of a stick up his ass.

Mrs. Eric Sinclair had been a society lady until her death eight years earlier. Seth laughed to think of anybody ever calling that powdered, pampered and perfumed lady a housewife.

Not that she couldn't cook, he knew. Her chocolate chip cookies were reputed to make a grown man beg from a hundred yards away. If that was where Erin had learned the recipe, then Seth knew from experience, it was fact.

Erin, their only daughter, borderline genius, honor student, graduate of Yale, was one of the detectives out of vice.

Why she had chosen to become a cop was beyond his comprehension, but she was a damn good cop, razor-sharp instincts, a good eye, and fair.

Those instincts were nothing short of miraculous. She could work a case like a terrier, gnawing and chewing at it until it all came together. It was uncanny, the way she could size a person up in barely a blink, know whether or not that person was the one she needed, or the one who would lead her to the one she needed.

And you couldn't lie to her.

Most cops developed an instinct about cons and liars and could recognize them easily enough.

She didn't recognize. She just knew, in a way that was downright eerie sometimes. That was how she had left her uniform behind so quickly, how she had become a detective after only two years on the streets.

Drumming his fingers on the desk, he continued to stare at her, a frown marring his features. Black, wavy hair tumbled over his forehead, and the scowl sat rather well on his poetically handsome face. His normally smiling mouth was compressed into a grim line, and his straight black brows pulled down over his deep, deep, brown eyes. High, chiseled cheekbones and a mouth that no plastic surgeon could ever hope to duplicate completed his face, a face that had started setting girls to dreaming before he even got to junior high.

Erin knew he was watching her. Hell, she thought with inner amusement, he had always watched her from the day she had left her uniform behind and entered the private sanctum of Avalon's small detective force. Even before that, she suspected.

Idly, as if just noticing his scrutiny, she glanced up at Seth and smiled at him as a shiver raced down her spine. Just looking at him — even after two years of being his lover and friend — just looking at him was enough to make her mouth water and her knees go weak.

His lids drooped slightly as one corner of his mouth lifted. Erin's heart starting racing as his eyes focused on her mouth before trailing down her neck and torso, lazily working back up again until he was once more staring into her eyes.

Something was bothering him.

Tearing her gaze away from him wasn't as easy as she made it appear and that hot, lingering glance had her insides jumping, though she kept a clear, calm mask on her face. Seth Porter had always had the ability to make her body do a slow, subtle meltdown.

He could make her laugh, make her crazy, make her needy. He had already made her love him, something she had sworn she would never do.

She knew him like no other could, even though she doubted he understood just how well she knew him. Erin knew that he wasn't happy with her, and she knew him well enough to know why.

Erin also knew, as much as it hurt, that there was nothing she could do about it.

She had no intention of getting any more involved with him. As much as she loved him, it wouldn't be fair.

Not when she had known, from the time she'd turned fifteen that she would die before her thirtieth birthday.

Mentally, she sighed. She should have never given in to him. It wasn't as if she lacked for male company. She had one or two friends who would have been glad to share a meal and the lonely nights with her, without her becoming too attached.

Attached? she thought, half-hysterically. *Is that how you describe how you feel, Erin? Attached?*

Erin could all but hear his muttered curse when she finally dragged her gaze away from him, returning her eyes, if not her attention, to the report before her.

Hurling his pen down on the battered, scarred desk, Seth shot to his feet and jerked his jacket on, automatically shifting the side holster he wore into place. Damn, it infuriated him the way she could shut him out, the way she could carry on during the day as though she hadn't spent the night whimpering and moaning in his arms. When he was fucking her — hilt-deep inside that tight, sweet, pale body of hers — that was the only time she ever showed any emotion.

His heart was on his damn sleeve for the whole world to see and Erin was able to sit there, making polite chitchat with their superiors as though she and Seth were mere acquaintances. While he wanted to throttle any man who so much as smiled at her, Erin merely chuckled with amusement when the ADA practically stripped herself nude and offered her small, lush body up to him.

He wanted marriage.

Erin wouldn't even consider them living together.

Storming out of the bullpen, hands jammed into the pockets of his rumpled jeans, Seth wished wholeheartedly he had never given in to the urge to ask the ice queen out on a date.

* * * * *

Seth collapsed atop Erin, his heart pounding wildly in his chest, his large body trembling and soaked with sweat. Beneath the length of his long, rangy body, he could feel the shudders that still racked Erin's subtly curved form, could still feel the aftershocks of her climax squeezing around him. The spasms that racked her body would linger and her pussy would hug his cock for long minutes before she was done, and Seth would want to fuck her again before it was over.

The pale skein of her hair was held in one tight fist, as he buried his dark, swarthy face in the hollow of her neck, breathing in the soft, sweet scent of vanilla and peaches. Cupping the firm, smooth curve of her ass in his hand, he groaned and rocked into her, grinding his narrow hips against her as she convulsed rhythmically around him, the hot creamy sheath draining him totally dry.

When her body finally stopped shuddering, his arms closed around her as he turned and shifted, tucking her against his side. Closing his eyes, Seth gave in to the urge to cuddle her close as he so desperately needed. She snuggled up against him as she always had in the past, but it no longer gave him the hope that she felt the same way about him that he did about her.

Damnation, he loved her.

"Are you going to tell me what's bothering you?" she asked quietly, tracing a path across his chest with the tip of her nail. Her lashes lifted slowly, revealing her pale blue eyes, warm and sleepy, as full of emotion as he would ever see them.

Catching her hand, he raised it to his lips, pressed a kiss to the inside of her wrist. "It's nothing, Erin," he murmured, dragging the scent of her skin into his lungs. Even as he lied, he hoped she would call him on it.

But she merely sighed and laced her fingers with his.

Frustrated, Seth disentangled himself from her arms and sat up, hanging his legs over the side of the bed, the cold floor beneath his feet, while he stared into the dark room. "Erin, I hate this."

Sitting up, securing the sheet around her breasts, Erin asked calmly, "Hate what?" But she knew. She had known before she had even heard him unlock her door that night.

It was over.

"Not being able to be with you every night," he said, getting to his feet. Snagging his jeans, he tugged them on before turning to face her. She sat in the huge bed, sheets tumbled, hair disheveled, her eyes clear and placid, steady on his. Just looking at her had a fist closing around his heart. "I hate trying to pretend that we are just casual acquaintances when everybody who knows us knows that's bullshit."

"Seth—"

"I need you with me, not just a few nights a week. Always."

Finally, finally, something broke that calm. The word always. Her eyes dropped away from him, and she tucked a lock of hair behind her ear. A sapphire stud glinted there, reflecting the dim light filtering through the window. "Seth, we've talked about this before."

Always? She didn't have always. She had only a handful of tomorrows left and he wanted always.

"No. I've asked before, and you've talked around it. I want to know why you won't make any promises, why you don't want me making them to you," he said, shoving a hand through his damp, tumbled hair. "I love you, Erin."

Her slim, pale shoulders dropped and she lowered her head.

"Damn it, can't you say it back? Just once? Even if it's just a lie?" he demanded, planting his hands on his hips and glaring at her. His black curls tumbled onto his forehead, the muscles in his chest still gleaming from the sweat of their lovemaking. Just looking at him made her body ache.

And she was pushing him away.

"I won't lie, Seth." *But I won't tell you something that will make it even harder for you when the time comes.*

Closing his eyes, Seth dropped down on the bed, sitting on the edge, staring at the hardwood floor. "I can't keep doing this, Erin," he said quietly, tiredly. "I love you; I think I fell in love with you that first night. But I want a life with you, not just a few nights a week, whenever it pleases you."

"Seth, it's not like that."

Casting a glance over his naked shoulder, he said, "From my position, that is exactly what it feels like." Rising, he spotted his shirt lying next to her silk camisole. Grabbing both, he tugged the shirt over his head, and stood twisting the fragile silk around his large, gentle hands. "You're everything to me, Erin. But I don't mean the same to you. I deserve better than that."

Silently, not looking at her for fear his resolve would break, he took his keys, slid his feet into his well-worn loafers and left, her silk camisole crushed in his hand.

Behind him, tears slid down her pale cheeks. Biting her lip, she held back the sob until she heard the door close.

Into the silent apartment, she whispered, "I love you, Seth."

* * * * *

Sitting slumped at his desk, he stared at his computer, the resignation letter neatly typed, spell-checked, all ready to print out and sign. All he had to do was hit the print key.

And give up what was left of his heart.

It had been nearly two weeks since he had walked away from Erin. Two weeks that had weighed heavily on him. Seeing her almost every damn day, as composed as the first time he saw her, while he looked like hell and felt even worse.

"I wouldn't if I were you," a soft familiar voice said from behind him, a small loving hand resting on his broad shoulder.

"Mom," he said, staring at the screen, tuning out the chaos around him.

"That's not going to make you feel any better. Only time can do that," she told him, squeezing. "It would rip you apart to quit this job."

"They need detectives everywhere," he replied, shrugging.

Anita studied him with gentle, knowing eyes as she shook her head and said, "Not like they need you here. And everywhere is not where you want to be."

"I can't take being around her all the damn time," he said through clenched teeth, keeping his voice low, even though he wanted to shout, wanted to tear something apart with his bare hands. "Damn it, it doesn't even affect her. Two damn years together, and she doesn't give a damn."

I wouldn't say that, Anita thought, remembering the look she had seen a time or two on Erin's face when she thought she was alone. But she only said, "So you think giving up a job that you busted your tail for is going to make you feel better?"

"I don't know."

Chapter Two
June 2002

The body count was racking up. Five dead women in less than four months. Closing his eyes, Seth leaned his head back, seeing the mutilated, abused corpses that were the handiwork of Avalon's very own serial rapist/killer. Lancelot.

God, the media. Who the hell needed them poking their noses into this mess? Of course, since one of their own had been the fifth victim, they were champing at the bit to nail the bastard. And not all for ratings either.

Seth wondered if Gloria McBeth would still be alive if she hadn't dubbed the grisly killer with that particular name, thereby calling attention to herself.

Lancelot had chopped off Gloria's trademark braid of long, silky blonde hair and used it to strangle her. After being viciously raped and sodomized, the death had probably come as a blessing.

Gloria's rape had been the most brutal, but she had fought, long and hard. The tenacity that had landed her the cop beat in Avalon had landed the cops something priceless. The psychologist had mused…"Interesting…I wonder why he made this fatal slip. He never has before. It would appear he is losing control."

Oh, he had lost just a little something during that last battle with Gloria.

Under her nails were skin fragments, blood, and tissue, signs of the vicious battle she had waged for her life. Evidence that would put the bastard away for life.

If we can ever find him, Seth thought, expelling a harsh breath through his nostrils and opening his eyes. On the wall in front of him were the pictures of five lovely women. Below each picture was a name and life story. Below that, the death story and gruesome photos of the crimes scenes. Two hotels, one abandoned house, and three private residences. Three of the women, including Gloria, had been raped, tortured and killed in their damned homes.

"Not exactly the most cheerful thing to be contemplating when you have a wedding scheduled, huh?"

The cool voice still sent shivers down his spine, still made him ache. Cocking his head, he studied the woman who stood in the doorway, her eyes full of pity and veiled anger. "No, but I don't think they give a shit about whether or not this cheers me up. They just want me to find the motherfucking, sick-assed, butchering son of a bitch."

"It isn't his mother he's fucking," she commented, a slim brow rising slightly at his tirade. Though she made no other comment on his language, Seth felt it all the same. That look of hers was worse than a slap on the hand or verbal chastisement any time. Too bad Eva —

Watch it, Porter, he cautioned himself, dragging his eyes away from her, wondering if there would ever be a time when he didn't look at her and yearn. "Is there something I can do for you, Erin?" he drawled, reaching for the lukewarm Coke and draining it, even though he didn't want it.

She had been gone on vacation for nearly two weeks. He eyed her pale skin. No tan. She hadn't been sunning herself on a beach somewhere. And she actually looked rather stressed, more than she had when she left. Erin generally didn't look stressed. That was too human for her.

"I had something on my desk this morning that you and Eddie need to see," she said, reaching in her jacket and pulling out a disc. "Where is he?"

"Running late. What is it, Kate Winslet's latest DVD?" he asked. "Eddie's got a thing for her, but she's not my type."

"No. Paris Hilton is more your style, I know," Erin replied evenly, her eyes staring coolly into his.

Lifting his shoulders in a shrug, Seth replied, "I prefer actually doing it to watching it. But then again, you should know that." Was that a shadow that passed through her eyes, he wondered?

He couldn't begin to guess because Erin turned away, sighing. Reaching up, she pressed her fingers against her temple, waited for the pressure to ease. As the headache retreated a bit, she wished she could ease the ache in her heart that easily.

The headaches had gotten worse, steadily worse over the past few months. A week after her twenty-ninth birthday. Because she was practical, she had gone to see her doctor and was told it was stress-related. The CT scans had shown nothing but a normal, healthy brain. She was given painkillers and a daily pill for migraines that she didn't take.

No point to it, really. Eleven months later, the headaches were nearly enough to lay her flat.

It wouldn't be a headache that killed her. It wouldn't be a tumor, or a hyped-up druggie looking to kill the cop bitch who had taken his stash.

It would be someone she knew.

With a forced effort, she shoved those thoughts from her brain.

This is not going to be one of my better days, she thought morosely. Her nerves were still raw from viewing the DVD that had been left on her desk. How it had gotten there was anybody's guess. Erin really couldn't begin to guess which was more painful, seeing Seth or watching that disc on her computer, the disc of a young woman being brutally raped and murdered.

He'd torn her apart; first with his own fists and the tools of the trade career rapists tended to carry in their rape kits. Erin had no doubt that the internal injuries would have killed the woman in time.

She hadn't been given the time.

Was she going to have to suffer through that? Did she have Gloria's courage?

Oh, God.

"Erin?"

Turning back to Seth, she asked, softly, sadly, "Do we have to be enemies, Seth?"

Raising one thick, black brow, Seth asked, "Is that what we are? Enemies?" One corner of that clever, elegant mouth lifted in a sarcastic little smile. "I reckon we are. But we have a little too much history for us to be friends, Erin."

"Old history," she added quietly, folding her hands in front of her. "You're engaged to be married. I seriously doubt our…history is causing you much distress."

"I never said it caused me distress, sugar," Seth drawled, propping his booted feet on the desk. Studying her from beneath the fringe of his lashes, he watched as she walked across the office and laid the DVD down on his desk. One hand rested on it, until he looked away from it and into her eyes. "You're looking kinda ragged there, darlin'. You coming down with something?"

Ragged, hell. She looked…fragile. Erin had never, in all the time Seth had known her, looked fragile. He hated that worry, and the tenderness, that was building inside him.

"Watch it," she said, nodding to the disc, sliding it across his desk with one finger.

Curiosity flickered and he took the DVD, sliding it into his computer. "What is it?"

"Find out," she suggested coolly, moving across the room to stare out the window.

"Holy Mother of God," Seth whispered only seconds later when Gloria's face bloomed on the screen. It went on close-up and the camera trailed down the length of her body. She hadn't been beaten. Not yet.

Her eyelashes were still closed and she appeared to be sleeping. The picture faded out and reappeared on a close-up of a man straddling her naked body. No audio, but the absence of sound didn't make it any less horrifying.

"Holy Christ," Seth whispered.

Erin closed her eyes, resting her forehead on the cool glass of the windowpane. Every vicious second had been imprinted on her memory. And she knew it would never leave her. Her only release was in knowing that the waiting was almost over, that it would be her turn to face the evil.

And when she died, she would take him with her.

That was the one thing that kept her from screaming in the night as the visions came with increasing frequency, increasing clarity. Never in time. Never in time to stop the one who was preying on the young, cool-looking blondes of Avalon's upper crust.

And never clear enough to see his face, to see any marks that would betray his identity.

Behind her, she heard Seth's breath whistle out between his teeth, then speed up in impotent rage.

Several times, Seth tried to fight down the bile that rose in his throat. The disc ended after thirty-five minutes. Spinning in his chair, he rose and moved across the small office, catching hold of Erin's arm and turning her to face him. "Where did you get this?" he asked just as the door opened.

Eddie tensed, recognizing the tension in the air. He closed the door behind him and came in, his hands sliding into the pockets of his blazer while he studied his partner and Erin Sinclair with curious, cautious eyes.

"It was on my desk this morning when I came in," she said. "No note. Just the disc." Dispassionately, Erin said, "She marked him. His right forearm had three gouges, pretty deep. He may even scar from them."

Yeah. Seth had seen the gouges.

And he had watched as her long blonde braid was sawed away, watched as the obscure figure in black viciously tightened it around her throat, cutting off her air until her eyes bulged, then releasing her.

Another rape.

Another beating.

By the time he finally grew tired of his new toy, Seth figured the bastard had kept her alive nearly two days, judging by the shadows that fell across the bed.

"He has a job," Erin said from across the room. "A few screens show a clock. There's a ten hour period on both days when he left her strapped down."

"How many times did you watch it?" he demanded. "This should have been brought to me immediately."

She turned away from him, staring back out the window, her eyes dry and burning. "I grew up with Gloria," she said quietly.

And then she brushed past him into the bullpen.

"Aww, shit," he muttered, pressing his thumbs to his eyes.

Eddie closed the door quietly behind her and turned to face his partner. "What's up?"

Eddie's ruddy face was pale by the time they had finished viewing the CD together. A cop for more than twenty years, he had hoped to do his time without ever encountering this kind of depravity. "Why did he leave it with Erin? And how did he get it there?"

"She was out of the office on personal time, gone for two weeks. God knows when he put it there," Seth said. As to why, he didn't want to consider that.

"She said she grew up with Gloria?" Eddie asked.

"Yep," Seth said, kicking back on the rear legs of the chair.

"We'll have to question her."

"Well, I think we can safely say, after viewing the flick of the day, that the perp is definitely male," Seth drawled.

"Cute," Eddie muttered, digging in his pocket for a role of antacids. "I don't like this."

Me neither, Seth thought.

"I mean, why in the hell leave it on Erin's desk? She isn't connected to the case, her history with Gloria was a long while back, and she's not with homicide." Tugging at his lip, Eddie turned his eyes to the pictures that lined the walls. The resemblance between the dead women and Erin hadn't gone unnoticed by Eddie. Studying his partner out of the corner of his eye, he decided it hadn't gone unnoticed by Seth either. "She fits the profile."

"We need to put a uniform on her," he said, a muscle twitching in his cheek. If he knew anything about Erin, it was that she wouldn't like that at all.

"Not likely." The cool voice that came from the doorway was much more calm, much more collected.

He should also have remembered how damn quiet she was, he thought irritably, studying the tall, cool-eyed blonde in the doorway. "You may not have much choice in the matter," he said.

One slim blonde brow rose. "Do you really think I'd have a hard time losing a rookie? Please. I seriously doubt you could keep up with me, unless I wanted you to." She strolled into the room, moving slowly, lazily, as if she hadn't just received a very nasty gift from Lancelot.

"Has it occurred to you that you fit the profile?" Seth asked, rising from his chair and glaring at her from across the desk.

Settling down in a chair, she crossed one long, silk-covered leg over the other. "When we were in school together, before we drifted apart, Gloria and I used to be mistaken for sisters," Erin said quietly, her eyes sad and distant. When her eyes returned to Seth's face, he saw a simmering anger brewing there. "Whatever the reason may be, he *had* a reason for sending that disc to me. And if he's set his sights on me, I'll be ready."

Not if, she thought, with certainty.
When.
"No."

Cocking her head, a slight smile curving her mouth upward, Erin said, "Seth, I really don't see how you have a choice in the matter." A sick feeling had settled in her belly after seeing the case file on the first victim. It had worsened with each additional one, until culminating just two weeks earlier when she had found out Gloria was the most recent victim. "I've already spoken with the captain, and the chief. If necessary, he's fully ready to use me as bait."

"Like hell." Seth was reaching for the phone when her voice reached him again.

Softly, Erin said, "He's done this before."

Looking up, he stared across his desk at her, his eyes dropping to the file she held out. "Take it," she said. "Fifteen years ago. I have a friend in Evanston on the force. He accessed these files for me. I used to spend summers there as a child. My parents had close friends there. I read up on the case files after our third victim. It rang a bell."

Lies. She hadn't needed to read up on the case files. She had accessed them, illegally, years before. Shortly after she turned eighteen and knew it was pointless to fight her future, to fight her…destiny. So she had taken them, memorized them, prepared herself.

Sick at heart, Seth opened the file and handed the enclosed duplicate to Eddie. Same profile, same method-of-operation. Death by asphyxiation, brutal rape and beating.

"Some kind of copycat?" Eddie asked.

"No." Lowering herself into a chair, Erin said, "The fact that the woman was strangled with a rope made of her own hair was a detail never released to the public. I don't see these as being copycat."

"You've been reading the case files," Seth said grimly, turning a page to reveal crime scene photos. Grisly echoes of those currently in his desk.

"Yes. We're talking about a man who has killed eleven women," Erin said. "Over a span of fifteen years. And…they're being killed in the same order."

"Order?"

"The first one, back in 1985, was Alice Jones, a bank teller in Evanston, single, blonde, found in a hotel two days after she was reported missing."

Seth's looked at the board across the room. Allison Monroe, bank teller at Avalon First Bank, found dead in a motel.

"The second one was a kindergarten teacher, Meredith Baxter, married. Found in a vacant house three blocks from where she lived."

The second photo on the board was of Mrs. Marilyn Beard, kindergarten teacher, found in a vacant house just a few blocks away from the school where she taught.

"God have mercy," Eddie whispered as Erin went on, ticking off the details, the similarities. Right up to number six.

She said nothing, waited as Eddie and Seth thumbed through the file until they came to Erica Morrisey, a narcotics detective with the Evanston Police Department.

Jaw clenched, Seth stared at her lovely face as he rose. Hoarsely, he rasped out, "You're the target. The psychologist contacted a friend at the FBI, a profiler. We've been warned he already has his agenda, and he will stick to it. We haven't had any idea what it was and unless something major happened, we wouldn't be able to stop him in time."

Seth's hand clenched and he felt the rage building inside him but he managed to keep his voice level. "You're the fucking target."

With a tiny smile, Erin said, "I'm the something major, it would appear."

"No," Seth said, his voice almost soundless. *God, that maniac getting his hands on Erin?* He felt the insane scream building low in his gut and shook his head vehemently. "No way in hell."

Her face sobered and Erin moved across the room, around his desk, until she stood only inches away. So close, he could smell the scent of peaches and vanilla on her, a smell he hadn't had fill his lungs in more than three years, not since he had walked away from her.

"We can't stop him. He will find me, no matter what we do. I am his target, and that's fact, not hunch, not instinct," she told him.

"What aren't you telling me?"

"Eventually, I'll tell you everything you want to hear," she said, unconsciously promising him. Someday, before it was all said and she was done, she would tell him what he had meant—what he still meant, what he would always mean—to her.

"But for now, you need to use me. Let me in on the task force, plant a tracking device in my fillings, whatever. Even try putting some poor rookie on my tail, Seth, if you honestly think it would serve some purpose. But use me. Help me stop him so he doesn't start this again in another seventeen years."

* * * * *

What choice did he have? Seth wondered later that night as he lay in bed next to his fiancée. Eva curled her tiny little body around him, one hand lying over his heart, her leg thrown over his.

But his mind wasn't on her.

His mind wasn't on the woman lying next to him, the woman he was supposed to marry later that fall.

It was on the sad-eyed blonde who had left his office after he had reluctantly admitted, even to himself, that this was a chance they couldn't pass on.

Hell, how many cops were given the chance to save the victim before she became the victim?

And he would save her.

Failing wasn't an option. Because if he failed, the next body he would be called in to see would be hers.

He didn't doubt that.

After damn near going blind over the files, he had come to the inevitable conclusion that the killers were one and the same. And nothing Gloria had done in the news, or hadn't done, had pointed the finger her way. She had been on his list from the beginning. Side by side with Angela Neally, the reporter who had been found raped and murdered in her home, only a month before the final, and most brutal, murder.

Rolling from the bed, he gave up on the idea of rest. No time any way. He wouldn't take the time to piss for the next month, if it would save Erin.

Padding down the stairs of the large cedar wood house he and Eva had moved into the past spring, he went to the telephone and punched in a number he had known for years.

When her sleepy voice sounded in his ear, the knots in his belly loosened. Would he have to keep her next to him until this whole thing was resolved? *Damn right*, part of him whispered.

And he would, if that kept her safe. God knows, that was what he wanted anyway. Erin. He had just wanted Erin, always, forever.

"Seth," she mumbled sleepily, "if you have something to say, say it. Otherwise, I'm going to go back to sleep."

"How did you know it was me?" he asked with a frown.

"Well, it could be because I have caller ID," she said, rolling onto her back, the silk sheets falling to her waist. Chilled, she pulled them back to cover her naked breasts. It hadn't been the caller ID. She couldn't see the view-box without her contacts. But she had known it was him. "Or it could also be because you're the only person crazy enough to call me at...2:26 a.m." Her brain was fogged from the pain killer she had made herself take.

She had to get some sleep.

Had to.

Just because visions had told her she would die before she saw thirty didn't mean she didn't plan to fight it.

"It could have been him," he said quietly.

"He won't call me." Even if he did, she wouldn't know him. He would give nothing of himself away until the day he chained her to a cold cement floor, until the day he broke pattern—

* * * * *

It hit her in a flash of silver, the silver chains biting into her wrists, the cold cement beneath her back. The gently sloping floor and the drain that lay in the middle. The drain that would carry away the blood and body fluids that would pour from her body and his as they killed each other, him with his knife repeatedly plunging into her body, her with the nebulous but very real gift she had been born with.

Laughter rang through the air, perfectly normal laughter, and a voice that she knew. A voice that was familiar.

I'm glad I waited for you. I'm glad she turned from me. You're more than she is, more than she could ever be.

Who? She could hear her own voice asking. *Who are you talking about?*

"Erin!"

The bellowing from the phone shattered the vision and it leaked away before she could catch her breath.

A short one. But vivid, so vivid.

Wearily, she sat up and said, "I'm here, Seth," only seconds before he could throw down the phone and call for a black-and-white. "I'm half asleep, but I'm here and I'm fine."

On the other end of the line, his heart was racing in his chest. "Don't do that to me, Erin," he muttered, guilt snaking through him as he heard Eva climb from the bed. "Hell, you trying to give me a heart attack?"

"No, I'm trying to sleep. Go and help your fiancée go back to sleep, Seth."

The phone clicked in his ear and he lowered it, stared at it even as Eva descended the stairs hurriedly, her small heart-shaped face worried, a little scared.

With a sigh, he hung up the phone and turned back to her, assuring her everything was fine.

But he lied. Things weren't fine, and he wasn't sure when they would be.

Erin lay curled on her side, staring into the darkness. A fine sweat covered her body and she wanted to get up and shower, to wash away the fine residue of fear the vision had left her with.

But she hurt too much to move.

She had counted, all over her body, how many times that knife had cut into her flesh. Or how many times it would cut into her, she thought. Fifteen times, fifteen times before she gave up the fight. Her body ached from the rape that hadn't yet happened. And her mind had withdrawn. If she opened her mouth, all that would escape was gibberish.

He would die, too.

In the vision, each time his knife had cut into her, power had streaked from her mind and flayed through his. Tearing it apart as he tore her body apart, until blood leaked from his nose, his ears, his eyes.

And he still kept cutting her.

Time passed and her ragged breathing slowly steadied, her mind stopped chasing itself in circles. She would take him with her. He would die, just as surely as Erin would.

But she didn't want to die.

Part of her was tempted to hop aboard a plane and fly away. Far away. She had money. She could buy a small, isolated house and never leave it. Mama and Daddy had left her with money, lots of it, and she'd spent so little. She had never made a home, why bother, when she'd die before she could enjoy it?

She could buy herself a new face, a new name. She was smart enough, sharp enough to lose herself in the wide world, to blend in and disappear. She could be safe. She didn't have to die.

But that wretched ability to see also showed her what would, or could, happen if she fled.

The murders wouldn't stop.

And the killer wouldn't be caught before many more women lost their lives.

And if she ran, she would see the faces of the lost every night for the rest of her life.

Pressing her face into her pillow, she sobbed.

Chapter Three

Seth left the bed before the sun rose.

Sleep had eluded him.

Eva had fallen back into the sound sleep of innocence, her face free from worry, her eyes clear and trouble-free.

And he had lain beside her with his mind running around in circles. He'd always followed his instincts, and they had served him well, for the most part. Maybe not as sharp as Erin's, but he doubted anybody he knew had instincts quite as clear, quite as sharp as hers.

But his had served him well.

And right now his stomach was a slippery, cold little knot of fear that wouldn't loosen. He was afraid. Part of him, his gut, told him to put Erin on a plane to somewhere, anywhere but Avalon. Somewhere she would be safe.

But the other part, the cop, knew that Erin was their best chance of stopping the animal that was not only killing women, but raping them and torturing them so horribly that death was little more than a sweet release. A cop, a sharp, smart cop would have a chance that the other women hadn't had.

Maybe.

He was going to bug her. Slip a little transmitter on her so that even if she disappeared, they could trace her. She may have been joking when she had made that comment about putting a tracking device in a tooth filling, but he was going to do it.

She wasn't going to die.

Seth wouldn't let it happen.

The results of a sleepless night showed on her face early the next day. Splashing cold water on her face, she tried to wash the cobwebs away. It wasn't even six a.m. but she wouldn't sleep anymore, so after she finished showering, Erin dressed in a pair of sweats and fixed a cup of coffee.

Taking it with her, she sat in the window seat and pulled out her journal and put her pen to the ivory paper, blanking her mind. Sometimes it surprised her, the thoughts that flowed when she wasn't aware—this was one of those times. When she looked down and read what she had written, her belly clenched.

Something has changed. Something doesn't feel quite so dark anymore.

I'm not sure, but I think it's Seth. Having him and Eddie— but mostly him—around, makes me feel...safer. More secure. Something inside me feels a little different. A little less afraid.

I think I have a chance of living through this. And it is because of Seth.

Seth is planning on planting a bug on me without me knowing.

Eddie is going to be the one to do it, today at lunch. He'll try to slip it into my purse, and another one on my body somewhere, I think probably my necklace.

The meeting with the chief is going to get ugly. Colton doesn't like Seth, and he doesn't want him on this case.

Seth's going to be lucky if he doesn't get fired before this job is over.

I need to talk to him, try to convince him to keep his cool.

Like he'll listen to me. He's a good cop — the best cop I know. But he's so damn hotheaded.

If I live through this, it's going to be because of him.

I need him here, not in jail or in the unemployment line.

Eva is going to leave Seth.

"Well, fuck," Erin murmured, her soft, cool voice sounding droll in the silence of the room. "Aren't those just the cheery thoughts I need to start my day?"

Eva leave Seth? Now that the thoughts were written, it was clear in her mind. It wasn't always that way. Sometimes, things came as visions, like last night, clear, like a movie rolling in front of her eyes. Others were misty and vague, not even true thoughts, more like an idea, or a hint of one, that needed to be grasped, molded and once she wrote it down, it became more real.

But now...she couldn't see what happened. The gift worked that way, sometimes. That's how it worked this time, thankfully. Erin didn't need to see the details of Seth's love life, thank you very much. But Eva was leaving Seth.

"Why?" Erin murmured.

Erin wished she hadn't asked.

The woman's voice came through as though she were standing in the room with Erin. "Seth, you still love her. Don't tell me you don't. You can't." Erin caught her breath, felt suddenly disoriented, and could, for a brief moment, smell him, that woodsy, hot male scent that was all Seth. She could feel his sorrow, his frustration, and his refusal to deny the truth, though that was what Eva wanted.

Lie, Seth, Erin wished softly. *Lie.*

She felt him jump, felt him search the room for her even though he knew she wasn't there, felt his awareness of her, and then Seth's certainty that he was losing his mind. She cursed herself and withdrew. That was the closest she had ever come to revealing to anybody besides her parents and the man who had taught her control, what she could do.

Seth stared at Eva's slim back as she walked out the door. She had woken not even an hour after he had left their bed, which had told him something was wrong. Eva was the type who only climbed out of bed when she absolutely had to, and then, she only talked after she'd gotten three cups of coffee in her. It was one thing they had in common. One of the few.

She hadn't let the tears he'd seen gleaming in her eyes fall, and he wished she had railed at him, kicked him, hit him, screamed at him. Done anything but be so sweet, so kind. So...well, Eva.

He prowled the room, searching for something to explain what he had felt. A jacket, a shirt. Anything. He had smelled Erin. He had felt her. He had heard her, for crying out loud. "Lie, Seth. Lie." Tell Eva that he wasn't still in love with Erin, was what she had been urging him to do.

He had heard her. And Erin wasn't there. He was going out of his fucking mind. And he had a raging, burning hard-on, the kind that only Erin had ever inspired. The kind that demanded he find her, fuck her, claim her, mark her.

And she wasn't here.

Flopping into the leather chair, he pressed his hands to his eyes and groaned, "Porter, you are losing your mind." He had to get it together. Had to. Eddie was going to plant a bug on Erin today, somehow. Without Erin knowing. They had a meeting with the fucking chief. And Eva had just figured out that he was marrying her to try to fill the hole Erin had left in his heart years ago.

Just figuring out, hell.

She had always known. Maybe she had just figured she could heal him, or he'd get over it.

Shit, Erin wasn't a cold. More like a cancer –the incurable kind, the kind that eats and eats and eats away at you until it's taken everything inside of you. He checked to make sure he had his phone with him. He didn't usually take it, but he had to be available if Erin needed to reach him.

Damn it, Erin, he groused, shoving out of the chair and out the door for his morning run.

The cool morning air felt good to his gritty eyes. He hadn't slept worth a damn. His shoes slapped the concrete, the damp air filled his lungs, and his blood started to pump. Eva was leaving. She'd take some time after court to come back and get what she needed, and she'd come back this weekend to finish up. Seth wished he had known what to say to her, but he hadn't been able to say anything beyond, "I'm sorry."

Eva had laughed and said, "Yeah, me, too."

The bad thing was—he wasn't sorry. A fucking, fierce joy filled him and he knew exactly why as he ran faster, and harder, circling through the wooded trail, taking a path he hadn't taken in years. Erin. He cleared the trail that ended just shy of her house, nearly three miles from his, in just under thirty minutes, chest heaving, heart pounding. She sat curled up in her window seat, outlined by the light.

She still cared for him. She needed him. She wanted him. He even suspected she loved him, as much as he loved her. Seth didn't know why she had kept pushing him away, but damn it, he'd been a fucking fool to just walk away. He wasn't doing it again. Whether it was what they had discovered with her life being in danger, or with Eva calmly pointing out to him, "Seth, it's as plain as daylight, you love her like you love to breathe. You can't stop," he didn't know.

Now wasn't the time.

He wasn't so stupid that he didn't know that.

He wasn't going to accept his fiancée's ring back and run to his ex-lover and pound on her door until she let him in, so he could pound himself inside her until they both died from the pleasure of it. But he wasn't going to wait too long.

He walked over to the police car driven by the uniform he had assigned to follow Erin and tapped the window. Lewis rolled the window down, red-faced at being caught in a daze. He had a half-empty mug of coffee, fresh brewed, if Seth's nose served him right. "Have you bothered to call up to the Lieutenant and tell her exactly how visible she is?" Seth asked nonchalantly. He was pretty sure the kid had. Jake Lewis was young, but he was pretty sharp.

"I did, sir. Her response was, 'I know exactly how visible I am, and how visible you are, Lewis. If anybody is going try anything, I doubt they'll do it where you would have a front row seat to see it all.'"

Seth chuckled and ran a hand through his sweaty hair. "Anything going on?"

"No, sir. She's been sitting there a while. Looked like she did some writing in a journal, or diary or something that she kept on that seat there. After that she's just been sitting there the past half an hour, drinking her coffee. Left for about fifteen minutes, and ah, brought me some coffee after I called her."

Seth ran his tongue over his teeth. He wouldn't mind some coffee. Wouldn't mind at least stirring Erin up a little. Then he laughed and wondered if it was possible.

She met him at the door, dressed in a sleeveless vest-styled shirt the color of the inside of a sea shell, a soft pale-pink, and tan pants, looking soft and cool and feminine. Nothing like a cop, Seth mused. In her hand, she had a cup of coffee that she held out to him with an arched brow and a bland look. "Are you going to run over here every morning to check on the uniforms, Seth?" she asked as he took the coffee.

He drank half of it down even though he was still hot from the run. The caffeine went singing through his system, even as the sight and scent of her went singing through his soul. Damn it, she was beautiful. He crowded her at the door until she stepped back with a sigh, sweeping her arm wide, and drawled "Come on in, Seth. Make yourself at home, why don't you?"

The bland little condo looked exactly as it had the last time he had seen it, when he had walked out years earlier, his heart still pounding, his cock still wet from the clasp of her satin sheath. It didn't seem to fit her, anymore now than it had then. Too impersonal, too bland, too cold. *Which*, he thought irritably, *should have suited Erin to a T.* But he always had the oddest feeling she was keeping herself from settling in, keeping herself from, well, nesting.

There were no pictures on the walls, very few knickknacks, nothing that said, *This is home.* Hell, he was a man, and he had done more decorating in his house than she had done in hers. He started to wander through the condo, while she watched him with blank eyes.

"Is there something you need, Seth?" she asked.

Not, "Is there something I can do for you" or "Do you want anything?" The answer to one of those questions was too likely to get her in trouble, and Seth slid her a small smile at her wording. But she still wasn't careful enough. He paused in his search of her condo to cup her cheek in his hand, staring into her soft, pale-blue eyes, stroking his rough thumb over the velvety surface of her full lower lip. "I need a whole world of things, Erin," he murmured. Then, before he could do something he knew it wasn't time for, he pulled his hand away and went back to pacing her home.

He had been wrong.

She had one picture.

Over her bed, there was a large framed piece of art that he had bought her only three weeks after they had started dating, and he had felt like a fucking moron for doing it. The lovely, long cool blonde had shown nothing more than an almost amused interest in him and he was buying her a painting of a nude faerie in profile, arms up, eyes half closed, her long blonde hair tumbling between her wings to spill down her naked back. Her small rounded breasts were lifted up, her pink lips parted. The faerie bore an uncanny resemblance to Erin, which was why he had bought it. He had seen it from across the street while out of town at a conference and had spent a freaking arm and leg on it, and nearly a kidney having the damn thing framed.

When she had unwrapped it, there had been tears in her eyes and she had thrown herself at him, her slender, strong arms going around his neck, her lips seeking his, her tongue thrusting eagerly into his mouth. They had made love the first time that day.

She had kept the painting.

He turned to study her, absently rubbing his stubbled chin, wondering if he had actually seen a flash of nerves in her eyes. "You kept it," he said quietly.

If there had been nerves, any and all signs were gone as she replied with a faint smile, "Why not? It's a lovely piece of art. Not every woman is able to look back at something a past lover gave her, and see herself." She glanced at the slim gold watch on her wrist and said, "It's getting a bit late. Don't you think you should finish up your run?"

"Hmm. I was going to bum a ride off you and have you wait while I shower," he answered, almost absently, turning back to study the painting. The sweat had dried uncomfortably on his body and he had already cooled down too much to run back anyway.

"Really," came her flat reply.

"Yeah. My car's in the shop and Eddie won't be in until late. Eva was going to take me in but…well, she had to go in early," he said. He turned and was walking out

46

the door. He caught sight of a cloth bound book peeking out from under the cushioned window seat. The journal. If it wasn't for that and the painting, this could have been a fucking hotel room.

"Well, then. We had better get going," Erin said.

He heard the soft, faint sigh.

She took a folded jacket from the couch after she had slid her shoulder harness on. The jacket draped so smoothly, so femininely, the line of the gun never even showed. "Are you carrying an extra piece?" he asked suddenly.

"Yes," she responded.

He moved up behind her, unable to resist and rested his hand on her shoulder. The soft, sweet scent of her teased him, and Seth knew he couldn't stay away much longer. It had been too long already. "I'm not going to let anything happen to you," he whispered harshly.

A soft, sad laugh left her lips as she laid her hand on his and squeezed. "I know you'll do everything you can to keep me safe, Seth. Why else do you think I came to you with the disc?"

* * * * *

She pretended not to notice when Eddie slipped the bug on her. His hand rested lightly on her neck for a moment. He had already put one in her purse and her car. Now there was another one on her necklace. If it would put Seth at ease, then she'd tolerate it. They sat at lunch, and she kept a straight face without even trying. After twenty-plus years of hearing other people's thoughts, after having unwanted visions and thoughts pop into her mind at the worst possible times, schooling her face was child's play.

Though she couldn't feel other people's emotions, she suspected they were half-afraid she'd notice. Keeping her face bland was not easy. Eddie was as jumpy as a rookie would be at his first bank robbery, his eyes darting everywhere, his hands anything but steady as he went back to pushing food around his plate.

Internal affairs material, he was not.

Seth sat across from her, talking foolishly about anything and everything to distract her and she smiled politely while she waited for the clock to strike 1:30. That was when the meeting with the chief started. And if Seth didn't watch his temper — *Stop it, Erin.*

"The media's hounding the police chief," Eddie said out of the blue.

"I'm not surprised," Erin said, lifting one shoulder. The tiny little bug on her necklace seemed to weigh a ton, even though logically she knew it weighed nothing. This one was just a transmitter, didn't relay any sound or anything, just her location. Not a bad idea, all in all. Eddie had done well, putting it in her necklace. Later they were going to try to talk her into a more permanent one that wasn't likely to fall off, or get taken off.

She'd agree, if they'd just ask. She didn't want to die.

"Gloria's father is an attorney, and the mayor's golf buddy, her mother is a doctor. Funny, isn't it? None of the other women seemed to matter as much, but now that one of the city's more favored children has died, suddenly the people in power are in an uproar," Erin murmured, shaking her head. Gloria. Her heart wept slow, bitter tears. If she had known...if. What good would knowing have done? Would Gloria have listened? Would she have gone away? No.

"He's going to try to point the finger our way," Seth muttered in disgust, shaking his head.

"Don't let him," Erin warned quietly. She waited until he was looking at her, until Eddie was glancing away — Eddie would hear the words, but he wouldn't remember them for long as she did something she wouldn't have normally allowed. She forced her urgency into her voice and tried to convince him. Not force, or coerce, but convince. She could control some people's minds, to an extent. She doubted she could control Seth, ever. He was too strong-willed, but he might think back and remember, if she pushed hard enough.

"Seth, don't let him make you angry. He's going to push, he's going to be ugly, nasty, a fucking coward and he's going to make it look like you could have saved Gloria. He's going to make it look like you're supposed to sacrifice me, take whatever risks are needed to catch the killer, anything he can think of to make you angry. I don't know what and I don't know why, and I don't care. But don't listen, and don't let him make you say things that are going to turn and bite you on the ass. I need you," she said.

Seth's head was spinning, like it did when he'd had too much whiskey, or stepped off a roller coaster after riding it for the fifth time in a row. Were Erin's eyes glowing? Had her voice just echoed inside his head?

What the fuck…?

* * * * *

"I'd like to know, gentlemen, why we still have no leads on Lancelot," Chief Colton said. He had big eyes, a big nose, a small mouth, a small head, and a large forehead. All in all, Chief Angus Colton was a very homely man. But he was also a very rich man, like his father had been. He was a smart, conniving man who had been a smart, conniving cop, which was why he had ended up behind the desk as Chief of Police in Avalon.

Erin didn't like him. His eyes lingered too often on her. He had praised her in uniform, hadn't done anything to make her dislike him. But she couldn't read him.

Hell, she couldn't read Seth either.

But something about Colton made her uneasy. He was a good cop. Avalon had actually become a cleaner city, thanks to him. Fewer drugs, cleaner arrests, cleaner cops. But personally, she didn't like him.

Everything about him made her edgy, made her feel wrong.

"I think we have a much better lead on him now than we did a week ago," Seth said calmly, hooking an ankle over his knee, resting his hands on the arms of the chair.

"That's because he gave it to you," the chief snapped.

"He didn't give us his hours. We know that he works a regular job. He has an injury, one that likely will scar and when he find him, we can get a court order for DNA testing to compare to the samples we took from Gloria McBeth," Eddie said, shaking his head. "He gave us more than he intended, because he was trying to scare Erin. He knew she'd give us the disc, maybe he didn't care. But we know more. We know he is white, he is a tall man, approximately 6'2", 180 to 190 pounds, lean frame, and from what the medical examiner said when he looked at the disc, he's not exactly a young man."

Seth snorted and said, "Shit, Eddie. I coulda told you that. He ain't popping Viagra yet, but he's not a spring chicken any more. He's probably at least in his fifties, maybe a little older, since he was doing this twenty years ago."

"I'd like to know how you discovered this perp in Evanston. That knowledge wasn't given to me in my report," Chief said coolly, narrowing his eyes. "And how are you so certain it's the same perp?"

"We've confirmed blood types are the same. O-Neg. DNA testing is being run as we speak. As to how we discovered—"

"It's commonly called police work, Chief," Erin interrupted without glancing at Seth or Eddie. Hopefully they'd get the clue. "You remember, don't you? Investigate, look for like crimes?"

The Chief's face darkened but before he could respond, she continued.

"We're running profiles," Erin said, before the chief could say anything else to Seth and Eddie. "We may not find anything. I don't think this is the average career rapist. But something may show up." A small, cold smile appeared on her face. "I can say, he may get to me, but regardless, I will be his last."

"He's not getting you," Seth whispered harshly.

"That's the whole point," Chief Colton interjected. "For him to grab her so we can grab him. We need solid evidence."

"Solid as in him taking her off the street, or solid as in him tying her down and beating her and raping her?" Seth snarled, shooting out of his chair and looming over the chief.

"As a cop, she's trained in self-defense. She understands the risks, and accepts them. She's to be wired and once we have enough evidence—"

"Fuck that—"

Erin slid out of her chair and rested a hand on Seth's arm.

"Erin is a policewoman. She understands the risks and..."

The chief's words trailed off, and he ceased to exist for Seth as Erin's voice, echoed inside his head, throbbing, intense, deep. *Seth, don't let him make you angry. He's going to push, he's going to be ugly, nasty, a fucking coward and he's going to make it look like you could have saved Gloria. He's going to make it look like you're supposed to sacrifice me. I don't know what and I don't know why, and I don't care. But don't listen, and don't let him make you say things that are going to turn and bite you on the ass. I need you.*

His head was spinning again and by the time it cleared, Erin was speaking to the chief in a cold, clear voice, the one that could make a statue's dick wilt. "I don't recall agreeing to put myself in a position to be raped, Chief. I am the target. Even the profiler you have consulted has agreed that this appears to be exactly what is going on. So you have one chance to stop him, and that is using me. But it is only going to be my way. Otherwise, I'll disappear. I'll tell you what I told Seth. You could try threatening to put me in a safe house. But you and I both know I'd get out. And you'd never see me again. Which means you'll never stop Lancelot.

"And perhaps I should make this clear — I will not lie back and become a victim while waiting for somebody to come to my rescue. I'll work with Seth and Eddie, and we'll figure out what to do. You haven't worked the streets for years, and it's not your safety at risk — "

By this point, the chief's face was blood-red and he was at the point of exploding. Erin arched a brow and Seth had to fight back the urge to laugh. Only Erin could so neatly emasculate the Chief of Police without breaking a sweat, and not have to worry about losing her fucking job.

Erin Sinclair was as likely to lose her job as she was to sprout wings and fly — the captain was her uncle, she had two cousins who were city councilmen and an aunt who was a judge. The Vincents, her mother's family, could have owned Avalon, if they had chosen.

"Are you quite done?" Colton growled.

"Not yet. You are the one who just insinuated I was to allow myself to be raped and beaten to stop a killer so I'd suggest you keep that in mind before you say anything else." She was putting her neck on the line to keep the chief's anger focused on her, instead of Seth. He wouldn't fire her. He had brought them in here, for some reason, to fire Seth. He wanted Seth gone. If she kept him focused on her, then Seth's mouth couldn't get him in trouble.

And right now, Seth's dark-chocolate eyes were dancing with amusement, so it looked like her plan was working. "I never said you should — "

"You said enough evidence. I know that all we really need is him. We have DNA. But something tells me a bit more than that, for some reason that is beyond my comprehension. You don't seem to want my help in the capture. You seem to want a victim out of me, for me to wait and gather evidence while waiting for backup." She saw the truth in his eyes and she felt her belly roll. "No. I'm telling this you this now. If it comes to me being trapped with him, I'm killing him. I go nowhere unarmed...ever. I. Go. Nowhere. Unarmed. He touches me and I get cornered, he dies."

"I want him alive," the chief said.

"And if he has me cornered and I think I might be raped or tortured before backup arrives, he will die," Erin promised, watching as his face turned blood-red and his breathing increased.

"Gloria McBeth's parents deserve to look at their daughter's killer."

"And I deserve a chance at a full life," Erin drawled. Then she linked her hands through Seth's and Eddie's arms and pulled them, forcibly, from the room.

Seth's amusement at seeing the bastard lambasted quickly faded as his anger surged back to the fore. He followed Erin out of the office, his head still feeling rather rattled, anger churning in his gut. He wanted to storm back into the office and slam Colton against the wall and demand answers, and tell him he was keeping Erin safe and that was what mattered. But he still had that odd, muffled feeling in his head, accompanied by a pain that increased with every step he took, and he kept hearing the echo of her voice.

Seth, don't let him make you angry. He's going to push, he's going to be ugly, nasty, a fucking coward and he's going to make it look like you could have saved Glori...

I need you.

I need you.

I need you.

I need you.

"Hey, man, you okay? You look kinda pale."

Seth shook his head, pressed the heel of his hand to his temple and shook off the trance-like state that seemed to have fallen over him. Eddie was staring at him with worried eyes, while Erin continued on into her office.

Fuck. The woman's made of ice, he thought when she didn't even spare him a glance while he tried to hold his splitting head together. *Why in the fuck are you surprised she doesn't care that you're going crazy?*

The pressure, the daze seemed to finally be receding as he stood leaning against the wall, eyes closed against the harsh fluorescent light. He was startled when he felt Erin's soft, cool fingers on his cheek. She pressed a canned soft drink into his hand as he stared into her unreadable eyes.

A mask.

Why did it always seem like there were two people living inside her skin? The cool, clinical cop who didn't give a damn about anything or anybody, and the soft, sexy, sweet woman he had fallen in love with...the one he had convinced himself didn't exist.

"Headache?" she asked levelly.

"Yeah." He popped the top on the drink and downed it even though the headache, or whatever in the hell it was, seemed to be nearly gone.

Who in the hell are you, Erin?

She heard him, clear as day, as she walked back into her office. She was lucky enough to have claimed an office for her own, even though the tiny closet didn't exactly meet her definition of an office. But she had her own space, and she could have quiet when she needed it. When Seth and Eddie crammed in behind her, taking up the two chairs she had managed to fit in with her desk and computer, there was no room left.

Seth dropped wearily into a chair, staring at her with dark eyes.

Who in the hell are you, Erin?

She sighed, wearily, rubbing the curve of her neck absently before booting up her computer. "Colton is going to see my butt fired if I live through this," she said grimly.

"You are going to live through this," Seth said through gritted teeth.

Eddie didn't comment on that part, merely laughed and said, "He won't dare fire Captain Vincent's niece. Even if he outranks the Captain, he won't dare. Shit, girl, half the city government is your blood kin.

She smiled and sighed again. "Fucking bastard," she said, too tired to even notice the surprise that flared on each man's face. "Thinks I'll actually let myself come that close to being raped?"

They spoke briefly about the chief, then ran some reports. Seth took a list, Eddie took a list, and Erin took the rest, but they knew it was more for show than anything else. Their man wasn't on this list. They had to wait until he moved on Erin. She looked at the other files on her desk and said, "I've got some other things I need to get done."

They read the easy dismissal and Eddie trooped out, but Seth lingered in the doorway until she finally looked up at him, a faint line of irritation between her soft, tired eyes. He said gruffly, "We need to talk."

"We just spent the past several hours talking, Seth."

"You and me."

"Why? Seth—"

He came back in, closed the door behind him and dropped his file before he came behind the desk. Erin watched him with wide, startled eyes as he dropped to his knees in front of her and buried his wide-palmed, long-fingered hands in her hair, staring intently at her as he slowly lowered his mouth to hers.

Oh, hell.

When she didn't pull away, his lips came down on hers with bruising, hungry force that took her breath away, his tongue driving inside her mouth. One hand tangled and fisted in her hair, holding her head still and steady while the other slid down her nape to her back. Bringing her to the edge of her chair and aligning her body to his, he spread her thighs and jerked her already wet, aching sex into contact with his rigid cock.

Erin whimpered low in her chest as he started to rock his body into hers, his free hand on her butt, holding her tight against him as he ate at her mouth. He caught her tongue, sucking it greedily into his mouth and she sobbed when he bit down on it before tearing away and jerking her head back. Working his hot, avid mouth down her neck, down the vee neckline of her vest-top, he used one hand to open the buttons.

He tore her bra open and Erin stared down at him as he caught one swollen, pink nipple in his mouth, sucking it with deep, hard draws, while he lifted his eyes to meet her gaze. One hand was still buried in her hair, holding tight, as he slowly trailed his other hand down across her abdomen. He pulled away from her nipple to stare into her eyes as he freed the button on her trousers.

"Seth..." she whispered shakily.

"I can smell how hot you are," he said softly as he slid his fingers inside her panties. He traced the hard, swollen bud of her clit and groaned roughly in approval as she whimpered and rocked against his hand. "You're already wet."

He slid his hand lower and plunged one thick finger inside her. He shuddered as she closed tightly around him, fighting the slow invasion of his finger as he withdrew only to thrust it in again. "Oh, baby, you're tight," he murmured, leaning forward to catch the fleshy lobe of her ear in his mouth. "How long has it been for you, Erin?"

She was silent, hardly able to think past the feel of him inside her, stretching her. He pulled out, pushed back in and Erin buried her face against his neck to stifle the low moan that fell from her lips.

He pulled her back, still using the grip he had on her hair, loving the soft, silky feel of it. He had loved seeing it spread out all over his pillow while they made love, loved feeling it on his thighs as she sucked on his cock, loved feeling it on his chest while they slept. "How long, Erin?" he asked, driving his finger back inside, and starting to circle his thumb around her clit.

"Seth," she wailed softly, pressing her forehead against his, riding his hand in near desperation.

"How long?" he persisted, adding a second finger. She squeezed tightly around him and he groaned. *Should have locked the fucking door, Porter*, he told himself. No. He didn't want his first time back with Erin to be in her office. "How long has it been since your last lover?"

"Three years," she whispered raggedly, her nails biting into his neck as she shuddered and shivered around him.

Three years. Son of a fucking bitch. He lowered his mouth to her ear, pushed his fingers deeper, more roughly inside her and loved it when she whimpered and bucked as he asked, "Are you telling me you haven't been with anybody since me?"

"Yes…"

She could have cried when the heat of his body left hers. She was cold, empty, aching and confused. The distant mechanical snick only further confused her but then she felt his hands on her again and Erin could have wept. "Hold on, honey," he whispered. She shuddered, her body feeling too tight, too hot, too small as he slid her trousers and panties off. She felt the cold of her desk biting into her back and opened her mouth to cry out but his hand covered her mouth and he rasped into her ear, "Shh, shh. Quiet, baby. Quiet."

He took her hand and pressed it in place where his had been, pushing it down until she realized what he wanted. All she wanted was his sexy, talented mouth on her, or his hands and…what in the hell was he doing?

She dimly heard music and realized he had turned the radio on and it was louder than she usually played it. And why had he turned on the broken little window air conditioner unit? Maintenance had been telling her they'd fix it for weeks…the overly loud hum of it filled the air as Seth slid his hot hands under her butt and lifted her…oh…

Seth parted her sweet folds with his thumbs and drove his tongue inside, starving for the taste of her after so long away. His cock ached and throbbed with his need to be inside her, wanted it so badly he could barely breathe from it. But not now...Erin's weak, muffled scream sounded like heaven to his ears as he feasted on her cream-soaked sex. He slid up, and caught her clit in his mouth, sucking the swollen, engorged flesh deep as she started to rock up against him.

He drove two fingers deep inside the wet clasp of her pussy and groaned against her, certain he wouldn't live another five minutes if he didn't get inside her. He stared up the length of her body, and committed the sight to memory. Her hand had fallen away and she was biting her lip, head turned to the side, shirt and bra still on, but open, framing her sweetly rounded breasts, the nipples hard and stiff. The muscles in her taut belly worked as she lifted against him, riding his mouth as he fed from her core. He drove his fingers in, shifting his wrist, reaching until he touched her deep inside. She climaxed against his mouth, and into his hand, a silent scream of agonized pleasure muffled behind her closed lips.

Seth lapped the cream that trickled down her thighs before he slowly worked his way up her body. He took her in his arms, groaning in agony as her hip cuddled his aching cock, but he held her tight anyway, the scent of her arousal and climax lingering in the air around them and making him even hungrier. "You haven't had a lover since we broke up," he whispered against her neck. She shuddered as he spoke and he reveled in it, in knowing his touch could still do that to her. "And I could fuck you right here, make you scream and sob and you wouldn't care, would you, Erin?"

"No," she sighed.

"We need to talk. Do you still need to know why?"

Her head fell back and she met his eyes. Her eyes looked warm, soft, and sleepy. He mused how unguarded she looked as she reached up and touched his cheek. "No," she murmured, shaking her head against his shoulder, touching her finger to his full lower lip. "No."

Chapter Four

Seth took the path through the woods that night. He cursed low and rough when he spotted the uniform in his patrol car, but the number gave him a little comfort. He went up to Jim Baker's window and tapped. The older guy rolled his window down and gave him a slow once over, starting at his hair and working down over the black button-down shirt, the black belt with a silver buckle and the black trousers.

Jim ginned widely and said, "I wonder what you're doing here looking so pretty."

Seth blinked once, his long lashes drooping low over his eyes as he flipped Jim off. Jim laughed, his friendly, hangdog face looking pleased. "It's about time," he said affably. "You know that Eva's a sweet girl, Seth, but she's not for you. You and Erin...now that's right."

"I guess I can count on you not seeing me here, right?" Seth asked.

Jim's eyes blanked and gave Seth a dopey look. "Seeing you where?"

Seth turned back to Erin's condo, his blood pumping hot and fast in his veins as he crossed the walk. He knocked on the door and waited.

Erin stared at herself in the mirror. She felt like a fool. A schoolgirl.

When he knocked, she thought she was going to jump out of her skin. The silvery-gray silk of the short robe slithered against her skin as she pulled it on. She hadn't been able to decide what to wear.

So she'd decided on nothing.

No dress seemed right.

And she'd never felt comfortable in lingerie, beyond the slinky kind she loved to wear under her clothes.

So she had taken a long bubble bath in water she had laced with oil. She twisted her hair around and clipped it on top of her head, and because she recalled it was something Seth liked, she removed her makeup, but slicked her mouth with a dark wine-red lipstick, that new kind that would stay on. She had just finished applying the glossy topcoat when he knocked.

She smoothed the short robe and walked to the door, pressing a hand to her belly, trying to calm the butterflies. She had burning candles scattered everywhere, telling herself it would calm her frazzled nerves, but Erin knew better.

She pulled the door open and met Seth's eyes, her breath catching and lodging in her throat. His dark eyes met hers, moved down to linger on her mouth before sliding down to move over her body like a hand. She returned his gaze, studying his lean body, the black shirt that spread over wide shoulders, his flat belly, the silver of his belt buckle winking at his waist. Her heart trembled in her chest as she found herself eyeing his massive erection before trailing down the long, muscled length of his black-clad thighs and back up to meet his eyes.

"Let me in, Erin," he said gruffly.

She moved aside and he came in, slowly, still staring at her as he closed the door behind him. He pulled his gaze away from her body and met her eyes, his deep-brown eyes hot and hungry. "Take off your robe," he whispered.

She reached for the silk tie at her waist and loosened it before rolling her shoulders and letting the silk fall from her body to puddle at her feet, all the while staring at Seth. He prowled around her, reminding her of a lion—lean, predatory, hungry. He stopped behind her and she moaned when he gripped her hips and pushed his cock against her butt, rocking there while he lowered his head to nuzzle her neck.

"Can we talk later?" he whispered against her ear, reaching around to cup her soaked sex in his hand.

"If you don't mind," she panted, spreading her thighs and reaching behind her with one hand, burying her fingers in the short wavy hair at his nape.

He pulled his hand from her slowly, trailing it up her body, so that the cream left a wet path on her torso. He finished his slow circle around her, stopping in front of her. "Take your hair down," he told her.

She pulled the clip out and the silvery-blonde tresses tumbled free nearly to her waist. Seth stepped up and gathered handfuls of it, groaning and lowering his head to bury his face against it. "I'm not leaving you again, Erin. We belong together, you know that, don't you?" he said raggedly against her neck as he backed her up. The counter that separated the living area from the kitchen was cool against her butt as he boosted her onto it.

"I know," she said, feeling her heart break inside her chest. *It's not fair!* She was supposed to be with him—so why did she keep seeing herself die? She reached for the buttons of his shirt and nearly ripped it in her haste to see him, the hard muscled wall of his golden chest, a light dusting of hair just between his pecs and trailing down his carved abs before thinning down to a line that disappeared inside his trousers.

He had already opened his belt and trousers. Erin gasped when his cock sprang free—thick, hard, full—the dark head ruddy, a drop of moisture beading on top. He moved closer, gripping her hips. "You know about Eva—" he said hoarsely, catching her reaching hands and pinning them down, waiting until she was staring at him. "I haven't been with anybody besides her in two years, and before we got serious we each had health tests. And she couldn't take the pill—caused her migraines—so I never slept with her without wearing a rubber. We weren't ready to talk about any kind of family yet, so it never happened."

He let go of her hands, but pressed them tight to the counter and then he jerked her hips closer, palming her thighs and opening her wide. "I wanted you to know that, because I'm going to fuck you, come inside you, not a piece of latex," he said as he started to push against her, his thick width stretching her. "I love you and I never stopped. One of these days, you will say it back."

Her heavy lids lifted, revealing her crystalline blue eyes, wide and glittering with hunger and need and emotion, more than Seth had ever seen, and she whispered roughly, "I can say it now, Seth. I've always loved you. "

His eyes widened, his pupils dilated as he stared down at her. His hands went back to her wrists, locking around them and tightening as he started to breathe heavily, his nostrils flaring, his heart pounding heavier, faster, as his cock hardened even more, to the point of an almost excruciating pain. "Fuck," was the only warning she had before he pulled out just a little before he started to drive inexorably inside, carving his way through her tight, swollen passage as she whimpered in pain and squirmed around him. Unable to stop him, she tried to scoot back, away from the heavy invasion and Seth growled. He shifted his grip, so that his arms looped under her thighs and knees and he could still grip her wrists and pin her in place as he thrust home. Nestled deep, Seth shuddered and rested his forehead against hers, the hot satin of her pussy clinging to him, her heart pounding against his.

*Fuck...at last...*he thought, holding deep and still for just a moment, reveling in the wonder of being buried deep within her again. But he could only revel in it for so long, as her tissues fluttered and rippled around him, and her words echoed in his mind. Her silky, creamy heat held him tight, snug, her tissues clinging to him in a sweet caress as he pulled out and drove back in.

He shifted and picked her up, taking her down to the floor, propping her knees on his shoulders, but taking her wrists and pinning her down again. He was fucking pissed. "Why?" he demanded. "Why didn't you tell me then?" as he thrust hard inside her.

"Seth...please..." she sobbed underneath him, tightening her pussy around him, unable to move.

"Why?" He pulled out and drove back in, moving higher on her body, so that when his cock burrowed back inside her swollen sheath, he was rubbing against her G-spot. Then he started to thrust shallowly, taunting her, glaring down at her, waiting until she was pleading and straining against him, unable to move anything more than her head. "Why, Erin?" he purred, sliding deep inside to give her one slow, lingering caress before resuming his torturous play. He let one of her legs go so that he could pin both of her wrists in one hand. He reached down and caught her clit, tweaked it, circled around it, waited until he could see that she was hovering right at the edge of coming, then he backed off.

"I'll keep it up all night, until you tell me," he warned her when she screamed out in frustration. "You knew it, knew that was all I needed to hear from you, and you wouldn't tell me. All I need to know is why." He slid his hot, burning gaze down the length of her pale body, to where they joined, watching as his cock slid between the full, pouting lips of her sex. He pulled out, his thick shaft ruddy, glistening wet from her cream. Pushing shallowly in, he pulled out and pushed back in again, balls deep this time, until the curls that covered his groin tangled with the pale blonde curls that covered her mound. He ground himself against her, feeling her shudder, loving her moans.

He reached down and caught her clit, stared at the swollen bud, hard and red and shining with the cream of her arousal as she clenched down, and screamed. "Why?" he asked, resuming his torture. But he had given her a little too much stimulation while he had watched his cock drive into her pussy, as he watched the play of his fingers on her sweet body and she started to come in slow, rhythmic milking sensations that squeezed and held his cock.

He pulled his cock halfway out and rasped, "Fuck it, Erin, no fair. You haven't told me why." Gritting his teeth against the urge to fuck her hard and come himself, he released her wrists and slapped the cheek of her ass as he nuzzled the satiny skin of the thigh he still had draped over his shoulder. He started to withdraw completely. She could go ahead and come and he'd let her, but damn it, he'd get some answers —

Either she had read his mind or his face was too damn open because she slithered up and wrapped both legs around his waist and moaned, "Noooo," as she rocked up against him, holding him deep inside, while the slow, pulsating waves of her orgasm grew stronger and longer. Erin came slowly…and it lasted forever. Seth gritted his teeth and tried to tell himself he could hold out.

Then he pinned her to the floor again and started shafting her, shuddering as he had to work his cock inside her, her pussy tight and resistant as she came and shuddered and pulsed around him, those sweet, intense milking sensations that gripped and held his cock like nothing he had ever felt in his life.

She threw back her head, sobbing with her climax, and Seth bit her along the exposed line of her neck. He nestled deeply inside her, rocking slowly back and forth as his own orgasm built and grew and exploded from him in a tidal wave. "Erin," he gasped against her neck, reaching down, finding her hand and holding it tightly as he pumped her climaxing body full of his seed, shuddering. He pulled halfway out as her body started to relax a little and pushed back in, pumping his hips, and growling roughly until he had completely emptied himself inside her.

He waited until he could breathe again before he flopped onto his back, taking her with him. "Every woman alive would hate you if they knew your secret," he whispered as he nuzzled her neck. "How in God's name can you come, and keep coming for minutes on end?"

Erin surprised him by giggling.

He lifted up, moving her onto his lap. Her hair fell in a sweaty tangle down her back. "You need to tell me why, Erin," he said gruffly, lifting her wrist to his mouth and kissing it softly. A faint bruise was forming there and he felt slightly sick to his stomach.

She pulled her hand away and stroked his cheek, his neck. "Don't," she whispered. "I'm fine. I don't know a woman alive who hasn't fantasized about having the man she loves take her like that from time to time."

Her head fell and he caught her chin and made her look at him. "Then why aren't you looking at me? Why won't you tell me? Why didn't you tell me?"

Her blue eyes were glittering, and Seth realized she was near tears. "I couldn't," she whispered roughly. "I can't explain it right now. If there comes a time when I can, I swear I will. But right now, I can't."

His face fell into grim lines. "I won't go back to the way we were, Erin. I want a life with you. A real one. You and me, together, one house, one bed. Marriage. Kids. I love you. You love me."

Her hands cupped his face and her lips met his as she moved to straddle him. She pulled his mouth to her breasts and he took first one nipple then the other between his teeth, biting and nipping until she was squirming and rubbing her wet folds against him eagerly.

He groaned as her vagina slid down and took him inside, wet from her cream and his come. Her ankles locked behind his back and she rode him slowly. "You asked me to marry you once," she whispered as her eyes started to fog with lust and need. "If you ask me again, not now, but when this is over...and it will be over...soon...I'll say yes."

"Now," he growled, pushing up into her, his palms curving around her hips, biting into her soft skin. His swarthy face stared intensely up into hers, gleaming with sweat, his dark eyes burning hot with hunger and love and residual anger. "Now," he resisted, digging possessive fingers into her ass, stroking and rubbing her intimately until she quivered.

She shook her head, her silken hair falling over them like a cloak, caressing his shoulders, face and neck. "When the case is over," she told him, then her head fell back as he speared up inside her harder, reaching down to rotate his thumb around her clit. She hummed her pleasure, purring like a cat when he bent down and caught a stiff nipple in his mouth, sucking it deep while he stared up at her from beneath his lashes.

Pulling away, he moved up to kiss her again and whisper against her lips, "Tell me, then. Can you tell me again?" He laced his hands through her hair and pulled her back so he could stare into her eyes as she lifted herself up and dropped back down, taking his cock harder and faster inside her wet pussy as she started to move closer to orgasm.

She smiled, a slow, sweet curve of her mouth, still painted that deep wine-red and she said, "I love you, Seth. I loved you from practically the...oh, damn...do that again..." He had slid one hand down and started to rub her clit again and her eyes widened with pleasure. "Loved you almost from the first. I'll always love you."

He groaned and crushed her mouth to his, pressing down hard against her clit as he pushed up against her repeatedly, until she started to come again, those slow rhythmic sensations that quickly pulled him into climax as well, until he was gasping against her mouth and gritting his teeth while the muscles in her pussy squeezed around him.

"I'm staying with you tonight," he whispered against her hair. Then he forced out a weak laugh. "I don't know if we'll make it in to work tomorrow, though."

"Tomorrow is Saturday," she murmured weakly. He was still inside her. A long, slow pulse echoed deep inside her vagina and she shuddered.

"Good. Maybe come Monday I can tolerate going a few hours without feeling my cock inside you," he said, rising and carrying her to bed.

He let her rest for a while, curled up behind her, his cock cuddled against her naked ass. She was so exhausted. He had seen the dull shadows around her eyes for weeks, the faint lines of strain on her face. Others who didn't know her lovely face so well wouldn't have noticed, but he had. He had worried, even if he had forced himself not to acknowledge it. So he let her rest for a little while.

But she rolled toward him after less than two hours of sleep and he awoke to feel her hand gripping his cock firmly, massaging it before she worked her way down his body and took him in her mouth. "Oh, fuck," he muttered, winding his hands in her hair and arching up into the wet cave of her mouth as she slid her moist lips back down on him. She stroked his sac with her cool fingers, wrapped the other hand around the base of his shaft and started to stroke a tiny, maddening massage.

She pulled away to lick from root to tip and then she caught the looser flesh of his balls in her mouth and sucked it between her teeth delicately, staring up at him over the flat plane of his belly in the silvery light that poured in through the skylight over her bed. The full moon was what had woken her, and she had lain there, staring at his handsome face, happy just to look at him again for a while, but need turned her blood to lava and she went down on him.

He used his hold on her hair to guide her mouth back down as he rasped, "Stop teasing, Erin. Suck it."

She slid his length in as far as she could, using steady slow strokes, picking up as he guided her with his hand, loving the satin smoothness of his skin, how thick his cock was, how he stretched her mouth wide. The smooth, blunt head bumped the back of her throat, slid down further and she swallowed, taking more and more before she slid back up, reveling in his groan as she started the motion over again. She could taste their sex, his come, her cream, dried together on his cock. She licked it off, washed him clean, swallowed him as far as she could. His hips started rocking up and he forced her head to move faster and faster until he cried out above her and then she tasted his come in her throat as she swallowed, forcing herself to take his cock farther inside, and hold still. He shuddered and both hands went to her head, holding her still as he pumped furiously in and out, his semen still spilling out from his cock into her mouth while he cursed and rasped out her name.

She was startled when he tossed her onto her back and covered her, mounting her roughly and driving inside her as he caught her mouth just as she swallowed his come. She loved the taste of it, but was pretty sure he wouldn't care for it. He didn't seem to mind as he fucked her furiously, his hands once more tangling in her hair and holding her still as he shafted her roughly. She was lifting up to meet him, hungry and desperate, needing him as much as he needed her.

She gasped for air when he pulled away to lean down and suck on her neck, biting the soft, pale skin. The thick ridge of his cock drove deep inside her as he lifted up and stared down into her pale eyes, her lips wet and swollen and red. Her spine arched, her nipples stabbed into his chest. He planted his hands on the mattress and drove into her, using the powerful muscles in his back, his hips and thighs—she wrapped her legs around his hips and lifted herself for each thrust, screaming and pleading and praising, "Damn it, Seth, don't stop, please, harder...oh, oh, oh...harder!"

He pounded harder, reaching down and grabbing one knee, shoving her wide open, shuddering as he looked down at the wet, open folds of her pale, glistening sex, the darker gleam of his cock burrowing inside. He found her clit by touch more than sight in the darkness of the room and tugged it, squeezed it, plucked it, and said, "Come, Erin, let me feel it...make me come again...that's it, baby...when you come it's like magic...you could make a fucking statue come when you lock down with that sweet pussy...do it again...that's it, baby..." He fell on top of her and pumped roughly as she started her climax, forcing his arms under her, burying his face in her neck while he held on for the ride.

He was shaking when she finished, when she let him finish. He could taste her sweet kiss on his mouth, but he tasted himself as well, and he groaned. "Damn it, you've turned me into a freaking lunatic, Erin," he accused, rolling off reluctantly. His cock didn't want to leave its sweet nest and raged at him. He forced himself to sit up and haul her limp body into his arms. "Kissing you after you give me a fucking blow job, sinking my dick into you every twenty minutes, I'm going to kill myself...what a way to go." He caught sight of his goofy grin in the mirror when he flicked the light on and she covered her eyes and squealed, "Hey!"

"We need a bath," he said.

He waited until she was good and clean before he decided to return the favor. After drying her pale, slim body, he smoothed her vanilla lotion on her body and spread her on the bed before he spread her thighs and lay between them. Opening her sex, he stared at her pink folds before glancing up the long, slim lines of her elegant body, over the curves of her breasts, the line of her throat, to meet her pale, glittering blue eyes. A hot smile curved his mouth as he looked at her with a gleam in his eyes.

She was swollen and still sensitive, sobbing by the time he slid two fingers inside her channel while he ate her clit like a piece of cherry candy, sucking it greedily as he fucked her into completion. Waiting until she started to come before he hungrily drove his cock inside her writhing body.

When she calmed, he started all over again, riding her slowly...she was begging him to let her come when he finally let them both orgasm nearly thirty minutes later. Then they slept.

Chapter Five

Seth couldn't sleep any more than a few hours. He was too fucking edgy. Erin was exhausted though so he slid quietly from the bed and prowled the condo before returning to watch her in silence for a while.

He found her journal while she was sleeping. He saw the leather book, lying there, like she had simply laid it down when she finished with it, the silver pen on top of it. He started to walk by it. But then he went back. He picked it up. Put it back. Gritted his teeth and swore in silence. Picked it up again, put it down and left the room. Then he walked back, got it and told himself he was a fucking jackass.

Within ten minutes, he was convinced Erin needed serious psychological help, so he was feeling better about snooping. She thought she was psychic, for crying out loud. She wrote down how she would dream something and later how it came true. Or she would be walking or driving and the knowledge was just there.

The woman he loved was certifiable.

That was okay. He could handle that. There were a lot of good shrinks around here and what in the fuck did he care if she thought she could see the future or read people's minds?

It was as he kept reading that he started to care — she started mentioning him, his cases, things that only he and Eddie knew. A burning started low in his gut, and the blood started roaring in his ears. There was an entry that was six months old, about a drug dealer Eddie and Seth had been watching. They had seen him arrive and they were waiting for another to arrive before they went any closer.

Eddie had left to go get some food and Seth was walking, stretching his legs. He never left the car during a stakeout unless it was to get food and he had left the car this time, for no good reason but he had done it. A quiet, insistent voice, like a low-volume version of the one today, he realized, had kept whispering "Get out, Seth, get out."

He never walked this close without being certain there was a reason. But the voice kept whispering, "Closer. Closer."

If he hadn't, he wouldn't have heard the girl's strangled scream before Pritchard cut off her air supply as he ripped off her denim capris.

She had been all of ten.

And Daniel Pritchard went from drug dealer to kidnapper and would-be child rapist in a heartbeat—Seth had taken his first life. Guilt wasn't something that plagued him at night, but the whispered voice in his mind had him doubting his sanity. It had taken him a few months to consign it to instinct and file it away.

It had been Erin.

No. Impossible. But as he kept reading, he read more and more that should have been impossible. And either Erin was suffering serious delusions, or it was all true. She knew another woman was going to die days before it happened and she agonized, but she never knew who until it was too late. Seth felt sick as he read of her guilt over Gloria and realized if she was this delusional, she may well be suicidal as well. If she really believed this, if she had really convinced herself of this, then she was holding herself responsible. He started to wonder if maybe he should talk to the department shrink.

Of course, whether the shrink was for her or him, he didn't know.

Because he wasn't quite certain she was crazy. He almost believed what he was reading. That made him certifiable.

He hadn't realized he had come to today's entry until he saw Eva's name. Although her name was at the bottom of the page it leaped out at him — *Eva is going to leave Seth.*

He hissed. He had only been away from Erin for forty-five minutes. And she had been pretty damn busy, her body smooth and oil slick from a bath and he remembered how long she liked to linger. The candles, the bath, simply the driving from his place to hers after she dropped him off would have taken nearly all of those forty-five minutes. Had she taken the journal with her? He had only just mentioned Eva. Had she heard from somebody else?

Something has changed. Something doesn't feel quite so dark anymore.

I'm not sure, but I think it's Seth. Having him and Eddie — but mostly him — around, makes me feel…safer. More secure. Something inside me feels a little different. A little less afraid.

I think I have a chance of living through this. And it is because of Seth.

Seth is planning on planting a bug on me without me knowing.

Eddie is going to be the one to do it, today at lunch. He'll try to slip it into my purse, and another one on my body somewhere, I think probably my necklace.

The meeting with the chief is going to get ugly. Colton doesn't like Seth, and he doesn't want him on this case.

Seth's going to be lucky if he doesn't get fired before this job is over.

I need to talk to him, try to convince him to keep his cool.

Like he'll listen to me. He's a good cop — the best cop I know. But he's so damn hotheaded.

If I live through this, it's going to be because of him.

I need him here, not in jail or in the unemployment line.

Eva is going to leave Seth.

That did it. She was crazy, he decided. He shoved all the logical reasons why he should believe to the back of his head. Because if he did believe, then it meant the impossible.

The impossible couldn't be explained. What couldn't be explained...he ignored. Seth closed the journal, fighting the urge to hurl the leather-bound book across the room. *She was crazy — it wasn't her fault. Of course, it was his fault that he had gone and read her journal. But all in all, it was a good thing —*

"I'm not crazy, Seth. Nor am I delusional, but, yes, it is your fault you read my journal." Her cool, quiet voice came from the doorway and Seth closed his eyes and felt blood rush up his neck.

"Erin, have you talked to anybody about these, ah...beliefs?" he asked, casually. Best to handle this calmly, quietly. He had to get her to understand the problem, so he could get help for her. The woman he loved had just gone and fallen off the deep end.

"Oh, I fell a long time ago, Seth," she said, laughing and moving out of the doorway. She paused and held a finger to her lips, smiling like a mischievous child as she removed her silver chain from her throat. Her mother had bought the hammered links for her, just before her parents had died in a car crash, and she never removed it...so that action, combined with the secretive *ssshhh* was a little bothersome.

Then she took her purse, dropped the necklace inside the bugged purse and carried both to the closet, wrapped them in a leather coat, effectively and completely muffling them. But then, she dropped the bundle inside a garment bag, and rolled the garment bag into a ball and carried it to the closet in the spare bedroom at the far end of the condo before returning, drawling, "We'd better have the conversation about my sanity in privacy, don't you think? I realize it was just supposed to be a transmitter on my neck, but I shouldn't really take that chance, now should I?"

Her eyes were bright and snapping and flags of color rode high on her cheekbones as she strode naked into the room, watching Seth closely. She spied his shirt on the floor and picked it up, shrugging it on and buttoning enough of the buttons to hold the larger garment on her slim frame. It skimmed her thighs, falling almost to her knees as she settled in a large, ivory leather chair. She stared at him in the dim light, her face still mostly in shadow, but he saw the play of emotions there and he wondered at it. Her face was always so blank—but her eyes were bright with anger, her cheeks flushed with it, a tiny vicious smile curving her mouth.

"Was it interesting reading, Seth?" she asked coolly, sounding almost like herself.

"Ah, Erin, maybe we should call Cat. She's a good doctor and—"

"Cat can go fuck herself," Erin said smoothly. Caitlin Devore was the police psychiatrist and normally Erin would try to be a little more respectful. But she was a bit pissed.

Seth's eyes widened just slightly before he blanked his features. Her normally perfect composure had broken. That ice-queen façade had cracked and Seth could feel the fiery anger that rolled off her in waves. "Psychics don't really exist, Erin."

"I'm not crazy, Seth," she repeated. "And I suspect you know that. Of course, I can prove it. And I don't mind invading your privacy, just this once, since you have no qualms invading mine."

She moved off the chair and crossed over to him and Seth had to bite his lip to keep from yelping when her cool hands cupped his face. Her voice slithered through his head and to his shock, he felt his cock harden as she spoke inside his mind. The touch was incredibly intimate, incredibly arousing, and his long body shuddered, his hands falling to the arms of the chair, curling involuntarily into the leather and gripping it tightly as his blood started to pound more heavily in his veins and his sex.

Why did he suddenly feel afraid of her?

Like she had before, that afternoon, that morning, that night six months ago...she whispered, *"Because you know I'm not lying, Seth. And people always fear what's not normal."*

Out loud, she said quietly, "The last time you slept with Eva was a week ago. She's been on her period and you've been rather glad of it. Huh—me being on my period never stopped us. You don't like that you've been seeing me around the office the past few days, with the case going on...you're always worried you'll end up calling her by my name while you're fucking her. You've done it while you sleep though." Her voice, always so soft, so cool and calm, was hot again, almost pulsing with her anger and when he stared into her eyes, they were flashing with it.

He recoiled, flinching with the knowledge she had just shared, unable to argue, knowing it was all too likely to be true. Erin's hands fell away and she retreated to her chair, curling her legs to her chest and staring at him. "I'm not a sideshow freak, but if you want more proof, I'd be happy to oblige. But if you're satisfied...?"

His gut churned, his eyes stung, bile burned the back of his throat. And he still wanted, more than anything, to tumble her down and fuck her until they both died from the pleasure. "This afternoon, you knew something was up with Colton?" he asked roughly.

Her lids lowered and she nodded. "I don't know why, but yes, I know he was gunning for you. He doesn't care for you. He doesn't want you on this case," she replied.

"What about after?"

She blushed. "No. I didn't know about that. It's not predictable, the way it works, Seth. Sometimes it's like a digital movie, with sound effects, a picture that will blow your mind, full-color, the works. Other times, I only get words, or thoughts, or just the knowledge. And I don't have any control over how it comes to me."

"Can you read anybody's mind as easily as you just read mine?"

"From time to time. Touch makes it easier. If it's something I need to know, then the knowledge comes. Other people have minds that are very...open. Cops don't. That's part of the reason I became one. And normally, I can't get a glimmer from you. You're one of the tougher ones. Your control is weaker now, from sex, from shock, from being tired. But normally reading you is like reading a rock." She smiled briefly. "That's part of the reason I agreed to go out with you, at first. I didn't keep getting all these random thoughts from your mind."

He just stared at her, trying to reconcile what he had just learned to what he had known, not even reacting when she walked by him. Seth just sat there, staring into nothing. The little girl, fuck, she had saved that little girl. She had known. How many people had she been able to help that way? How many of the cops he worked with? He knew all too many of the cases they had that seemed impossible and suddenly, an odd, almost miraculous break came. And he wondered how many of them were miraculous, and how many were Erin.

She returned a few minutes later, wearing sand-washed silk pajamas and a robe, offering him his shirt. "You're welcome to take my car," she said, gesturing to the keys.

His eyes traveled from the hand that held his shirt, up to her elbow, her shoulder, her neck, until he reached her face. "Are you telling me to go?" he asked gruffly, a hot slippery ball of fear in his gut. *Fuck, had he pissed her off that much?*

"Don't you want to?" Erin asked with a sigh. She had shored up her own defenses and felt her face falling into its familiar blank lines. Already, she had felt his fear, felt his confusion. Soon his rejection would come, and she didn't want to feel it.

When his hand closed over hers and pulled the shirt away, tossing it aside, she met his eyes.

"No," he rasped, rising from the chair to back her up against the wall. His hands cradled her face and she shuddered as she felt the massive onslaught of thoughts that battered her mind.

"No," he repeated, sliding his hands inside her pajamas pants and stripping them off. "I love you. I think I'd like it better if you were insane, but—"

His mouth covered hers and Erin's whole world shifted as she allowed him to touch her for the first time without her defenses in place. Shielding herself was automatic, was instinct, and it was more difficult to let them down than to hold them up. Without the shields, the thoughts that would batter her mind out in the real world would be too much, and she very likely would go insane from it all, but here, with Seth, just Seth, all she felt was what he felt.

And he felt only her.

His hands slicked over the smoothness of the silk pajama top she had pulled on to cover herself from him and he hated it. He jerked it from her body while he fought to free his cock from his trousers, fumbling and swearing, and Erin felt the ravenous need that filled his mind and just that was enough to make a long, slow pulse shudder through her vagina, enough to make her clit swell in anticipation. He groaned her name against her mouth as he freed himself and thrust home, arching his hips and driving deep. She pushed back and screamed, feeling the echo of how she felt around him, tight, wet, silky. He felt hot, huge, hungry as he started to pump his hips, working his cock in and out of her as he kissed her desperately.

She caught his face in her hands and felt something damp on his cheeks, startled to find something else in his mind, a gut-deep fear that she would have thrown him out again, that he would have lost her. She pulled her mouth from his, gasping as he circled his hips against hers and rubbed against her clit as she murmured, "No, I'm not leaving. You're not leaving…God willing, we'll grow old and die together."

Seth's eyes stared into hers, as he drove harder and harder into her, pushing higher, until she was mewling and whimpering and begging. She felt the backlash of his own pleasure in her mind and it was devastating, the force of it constricting her lungs until she could hardly breathe from it. "Seth, please," she gasped as he rubbed her clit, burying his cock inside her pussy to the balls and rocking against her.

She cried out, arched when his other hand cupped her ass and one long finger stroked the dark crevice there. Her head fell back and her lids drifted closed and his voice rasped out, "Don't close your eyes, look at me, Erin." She forced her lids to open and she slid her hands down, locking her fingers behind his neck, bringing her legs up and hooking her ankles over his firm, muscled ass, riding him a little, grinding her pelvis against his as he stroked her anus beguilingly, guiding her headlong into orgasm.

She screamed, short, sharp screams that fell in staccato bursts from her mouth when he started to press his finger against the tight ring of muscle, then entered her ass, and she came hard and vicious. Locking down on him, she rubbed herself against him like a hungry little cat as he growled and crushed her against the wall, forcing his finger deeper inside the virgin chamber of her ass and fucking her pussy hungrily. The rhythmic pulses of her orgasm milked his cock intensely, drawing his balls tighter and tighter until he flooded her silky wet sheath with a groan. Seth slid to his knees, still holding himself inside her, still pumping his come into her taut little body, feeling the tight, clinging walls of her ass holding his finger while she came around him.

When her breathing slowed, she kissed him again and whispered weakly, "I won't ever leave you, if I can help it."

Something was dancing around in the back of his brain, keeping him from sleeping. Erin slept like the dead. She had curled into him after the final time and whispered, "I haven't felt safe for months."

"Sleep, baby," he murmured, stroking her hair. "I won't let anything happen to you."

Months. He would bet she hadn't slept since the first murder had happened.

She had known. For how long, he didn't know. But Erin had known, for a good long while, that she was the target. She had been looking tired, more drawn, more on edge for months. He had noticed it more than a year ago.

The past few months, a handful of others had noticed.

He stayed wrapped around her body as the hours passed, holding her while she slept. How long had she known?

And what the fuck had she meant...God willing?

"You're thinking so loudly, even somebody who isn't psychic would hear you," Erin murmured as she roused from the soundest sleep she had slept in months. Maybe years. The arm around her waist held firm and she knew he hadn't slept.

"How long have you known he's after you?"

"Well, why beat around the bush?" she asked drolly, tongue in cheek.

"How long, Erin?"

She sighed, and squirmed around to face him. Staring into his dark face, reaching up and brushing the tumbled black curls from his face, she queried softly, "Truth?"

"Yeah. Truth."

"Since I was fifteen," she said, watching as his face went slack, first with failure to understand. Then with shock. Then it tightened.

"I think you need to explain," he said tightly.

"I had a dream, or a vision," she said softly. "When I was fifteen. My parents almost had to have me committed. They knew about the gifts. Mom had them as well. Dad did, too. Not as strong as Mom and I, but they were there. I was the strongest, and the clearest. The dream…I woke up screaming one morning, I had seen blood, puddles and puddles of it, and my body hurt, so badly I could hardly breathe. They called Josiah Hartman, the man who helped train me. I had such a strong gift of receiving, they needed help with teaching me to shield.

"Josiah took nearly a day to get here. He had to fly from London. By then, I was nearly catatonic. Josiah is empathic, which is why he was able to teach me shielding and Mom couldn't. Mom could project, and she could read minds but only through contact. When he touched me, he started crying. He knew my shields, knew how to get through, and Mom didn't.

"My dream had told me I'd die before I was thirty. A serial killer would stalk and kill me. But I'd kill him as well."

Seth felt the scream building inside him and knew he couldn't keep it in. Erin moved closer and laid her lips against his. Just touching, not kissing. "That's why I did what I did, and never told you, Seth. I don't want to die, and I plan on fighting, but I thought, at the time, it would make it easier on you," she whispered. As she spoke, she projected, like she had before, her voice sweeping into his mind, along with her emotions, and he felt her love, her sorrow, her determination to live. "It was a wrong choice, maybe. But at the time, it was the one I had to make."

"I'm not walking away from you again," he rasped, rolling and pinning her under him. "And you're not going to die."

She smiled, shifted the hands he pinned so that her fingers laced with his. "And that's why I did what I did at the meeting. I touched your mind then, but you already know that. I need you, Seth. You're the one person I can count on..." Her eyes widened, then closed as she felt his cock parting, then sliding past the lips of her sex. She was morning damp, but hardly wet enough to take him and she bit her lip as he pulled his cock out, and started to work it back in.

Seth groaned as he stared into her eyes, feeling the clinging of her sex on his rigid shaft, the discomfort on her face as he forced his cock into the swollen sheath he hadn't prepared. "I'm not losing you," he muttered as he pulled out, and went down on her, driving his tongue inside her, lubricating her, catching her clit and rolling it on his tongue, licking and sucking it until her fingers were locked in his hair and she was rocking her hips against his face, riding his mouth, and moaning.

"Are you here with me?" he thought to her.

"Yes," she groaned, pushing herself harder against him.

"I'm not losing you, not now. Not ever. Sweet, sweet Erin,love your taste." He felt her body's response to what he felt and thought as he slid his fingers inside her sheath, wetting them with her cream before sliding them lower to probe her ass. Lifting up, he stared up at her over the length of her body as he murmured, "I wanted to take you here, before. But not cool, collected Erin. She was too much a lady, too calm, too controlled. But you're not, are you?"

"Seth!" she shrieked, pushing up against him and sobbing as he slid one finger inside the tiny, hot little rosette, a sharp burning pain streaking through her groin and up her belly as he licked and sucked her clit.

"Push, Erin."

She did, with a cry, and he slid his finger easily inside and started to thrust it shallowly, moving his mouth and driving his tongue inside the sweet well of her pussy while he finger-fucked her ass. *"I can't lose you, Erin,"* he thought desperately. *"You're my life, my heart, my soul."*

"Damn it, Seth, please," she wailed and then her body stiffened and she shivered as the climax built and broke over her, her cream flooding from her pussy and he hummed with greedy pleasure, lapping it from her folds and thighs, thrusting his finger in and out, while she moved against him, riding his hand through the orgasm.

He crawled back up her body, his face gleaming with her cream, his eyes wild and hungry. He grasped her thigh with one hand and lifted it high, opening her still shuddering body as he started to possess her. "I can't lose you," he rasped. "Which means we'll stop him."

She whimpered and pushed up, her hot, swollen folds closing over the head of his cock hungrily. He buried his face in her neck and whispered, "Cool and collected, my ass," as he started to ride her hard. Catching her hands and pinning them over her head, he lifted her up so he could stare down into her lovely, bewitching face, her pale eyes nearly silver, damp with tears, her lips swollen, a tiny drop of blood from where she had bitten them when she came.

He buried his cock to the hilt and rolled onto his back, releasing her hands and commanding roughly, "Ride me, Erin." She planted her hands on his chest, staring down into his face. Curling her fingers into the firm wall of his pecs and smiling a cat's smile, she started to roll her hips, slowly.

She straightened, one hand going up to cup a breast, pinching a rosy nipple that was already peaked and hard, the other going down to stroke her swollen clit. "No," she purred in agreement. "Not cool and collected." She rocked her hips, feeling the head of his cock bump the mouth of her womb and she groaned in pleasure, licking her lips.

Seth stared at her, at the play of her long slim fingers on her swollen red clit, on her nipples, first one then the other, the dash of her pink tongue across her lips, her silvery hair falling around her shoulders, shifting to hide her breasts. She'd toss her head, and the silvery-blonde strands would slither behind her shoulders briefly, then slide down so that her red nipples would peak out at him.

He'd never seen anything so fucking erotic in his life.

He reached down, caught the hand she was using to play with herself and brought it to his mouth, licking it clean as he used his thumb to circle her clit and urge her to orgasm. She pouted and said, "My way. You make me come too fast."

"You've never come fast in your life, Erin," he said through gritted teeth, arching his back and driving his cock up into her. She tried to pull off and he grabbed her thighs with steely hands, holding her still as he started to drive up inside her, staring into her face. "Mine, you're mine. No man touches you, no man hurts you. I'll destroy him."

She fell against him, sobbing as his cock rammed against her cervix, his hands going to her ass and pulling the cheeks apart. The foreign caress of air on her made her gasp and then she whimpered as he rolled his hips against her and started to come, his come pulsing deep inside her, setting her own orgasm off. "Told you," he groaned when she was still coming around him, minutes later, long after he had emptied himself into her.

"Tell me everything, all of it, and tell me now," Seth said as they sat down over pizza. He had made her dress before he agreed to cook it, knowing he couldn't cook a damn thing with a naked Erin in the house. And since it would appear she really wasn't crazy and her life was really at stake, he had to figure out what they were going to do.

"There's not much to tell," she said as she sat down. Gingerly. She hurt. After having him pound into her more than half the night, why wouldn't she? "I know him, somehow. But I can never see his face. And I won't recognize him until it's too late."

She took another bite and swallowed before she grinned at Seth. "I missed your cooking almost as much as I missed you," she told him.

He smiled halfheartedly, and wished he could enjoy the playful nature she was willing to show him now, but he couldn't. He couldn't even think about eating and she was already scarfing down her second piece. "How can you eat?"

She arched a brow. "I open my mouth, bite and chew. Then I swallow. It 's a pretty handy talent, but not all of us can do it," she replied, straight-faced.

Then she slid out of her chair and walked over to him, wrapping her arms around him. Leaning her head on his chest, she cuddled against him, listening to the steady, soothing sound of his heart for a long moment before she said, "For the past year, I've had headaches, bad ones. I knew what it was. I saw a doctor, just to make sure, but it was just knowing what was coming. Stress, pressure, fear. I've felt like a thundercloud has been hanging over my head, and there was nothing I could do about it. I'm never hungry, I rarely sleep anymore. I never want to leave the house, and I can hardly focus on anything. I don't feel safe, no matter where I go or what I do."

"But it feels like it's gone now. I woke up this morning wrapped in your arms, felt you pressed up against me, and I felt safe. I felt protected. And not just while you were here, with me. I've got this feeling, inside my heart, and inside my head, that you can keep me safe. This gut fear started lessening the minute I gave you the disc," she told him, sliding her hands under his shirt and stroking the firm muscles of his back, rubbing her cheek against the vault of his chest. "You're it, Seth. You're what will get me through this."

"Even if I do get grabbed, you're there. You'll get me through this," she murmured, stroking her hands down his neck.

"I'm not letting a fucking murderer get his hands on you," he growled. "I'm putting a transmitter of my own on you. Damn it. This isn't enough."

"Yes, it is."

* * * * *

Seth stole the transmitter. Late Monday, he waited until nightfall to go to her house, and he walked around back and came in through her kitchen window, where she sat drinking a glass of wine and reading a romance. He glared at her and said, "I've been reduced to stealing government property, you know."

She smiled beatifically at him and fluttered her lashes. "You've been dying to steal something again, you reformed rogue," she said. "How come you're haunting my back door?"

Lowering his lids, he murmured, "You've no idea what I want to do to your back door."

Briefly, she looked blank and then she flushed, her eyes going glassy while the nipples under her shirt went tight and hard. He chuckled roughly before he said, "Habit. Don't wanna keep the same routine."

She had been starving and had settled for some cold pizza but she was already hungry again. "Where are we going to put it?" she asked. She had hidden her purse again, and the radio was playing loudly to drown out their voices. She wouldn't have been surprised if her house was bugged. Doubted it, but it wouldn't have surprised her.

He flashed the pair of simple silver studs at her with a cocky grin. "Us guys rarely notice a woman's jewelry until you're making us buy it," he told her. "These were added to the inventory by a cop chick—" he threw that in just to watch her eyes narrow. After so long of watching no emotion on her face, it stunned him to realize just how much she had hidden behind that cool mask and cooler eyes. He moved up to her, brushed her hair aside and fastened the studs in the upper holes of her lobes. "The right stud is the transmitter. If—" he blew out a breath and said, "When he takes you, try to lose the left one right away, then lose the right one in the car, or swallow it if you have to." He took his time smoothing her hair down, an unusual amount of time stroking it down her breasts.

She slid him a look from under her lashes. "You've a fetish for my hair, don't you?" she asked softly.

"If you only knew," he groaned. He gently urged her to her knees, watching her closely. "I've had entire fantasies spun around your hair, holding you like this, while you—yeah, that's the one," he murmured as she undid his trousers and freed his cock, taking his steely length in hand and closing her mouth over the tip while he wrapped the long length of her hair around his hand and wrist, using it to guide her movements.

She watched him, staring up the long length of his body through the fringe of her lashes, meeting his dark, hypnotic eyes as she slid her head down slowly, stroking the taut skin of his testicles with her free hand while she massaged the base slowly and firmly in time with the downward strokes of her mouth.

Seth groaned roughly, fisting his hand tighter in the pale silk of her hair and pushed his cock deeper, rocking forward on his heels, uncaring that the kitchen light was on, that the curtains hadn't been drawn, that any-fucking-body could see. He clamped both hands around her head, staring down at her, into her soft blue eyes, watching as he pushed his dark, thick sex between the rose of her lips, shuddering at the sight of her on her knees, staring hungrily up at him.

His cock jerked and throbbed in the embrace of her mouth as he drove fast and rough into her, until his sac tightened and he exploded into the back of her throat.

He sagged and let himself go to his knees in front of her, laughing weakly. "You know, that's one of the few times I've been able to finish an orgasm without you drawing it out forever. Every time I come inside you—" he cupped his hand over her wet cleft and ground his heel against her, "you milk me dry and keep on going with those infinite, forever climaxes of yours."

He jerked her loose cotton pants down and turned her onto her knees, forcing her to bend forward. It opened her wet, glistening folds, exposed the pucker of her ass. Seth groaned hungrily, pressed his thumb to the rosette and swore. He would have to wait for that—they had never done anything to prepare Erin for that, and they had none of what they needed.

"I need you," he rasped in apology, driving deep inside, gripping her hips and pushing forward. He reached out, hesitantly, wanting the touch he had felt when she had sifted through his mind and he found her, almost like she waited. The blood in his body seemed to boil as they sank into each other, their skin dissolving. He rode her body to the floor, rough and hard, hungry, as their minds and souls merged.

"Sorry? For needing me like I need you?" she whispered, twining her very soul with his as he pounded his cock deep inside, the head butting against her womb until she was shrieking with the painful pleasure of it.

"I love you," he growled against her neck, arching his head around until their mouths met and he could drive his tongue deep inside her sweet mouth, down her throat. His long, powerful body bucked and surged inside hers helplessly as she responded in kind, directly into his mind, "I love you, Seth."

* * * * *

Erin shook her head as Seth tried to tell her he would come over that night. She absently stroked the earring in her left ear. They had checked it earlier that day, coming into work separately, she in her own car, Seth returning to his house alone, creeping out at dawn, through the back way, and catching a ride with Eddie. He had watched through the tracking device, checking and double checking.

Now they just had to wait.

"What's the point if you are with me every second? Do you think he doesn't know? We've checked for listening devices, but somehow, he knows," she murmured directly into Seth's ear as he tried to find an argument. Of course, there wasn't one.

So he retreated to his house alone. Slept fitfully. And when Erin didn't come in to work the next morning he wanted to howl.

Chapter Six

She was gone. Seth walked into the condo mid-morning the next day and felt the emptiness. The rookie assigned to watch her was in the hospital. One of the tenants in another condo had found him while out running in the woods, the rookie unconscious and bloodied at the back of his head. Blunt force trauma. Like the butt of a gun.

But it had been more than the rookie not checking in that had bothered Seth. Something was off. Erin was in trouble. Somehow, since they had gotten back together over the weekend, some sort of bond had been forged between them. He had never thought he would believe in psychic skill, or in magic. And maybe it was just the love, but there was some sort of bond, and he knew in his heart, that the killer had her.

His hands were shaking as he got the transmitter out of the briefcase he had started to carry. And a sick feeling settled in the pit of his belly. The transmitter wasn't working. He shook it. Checked it. "Son of a fucking bitch!" he snarled, as he forced himself to carefully lay it down.

Even though he wanted to hurl it. If he did that, and smashed it, then he was fucked. If he had to, then he'd get Eddie. Eddie could fix anything. But first—

"*Seth.*"

He felt her touch his mind and thought he'd sob with relief. But right after he felt her touch, he felt her pain. He stumbled and went down onto the ivory carpet in her living room, and saw the room through her eyes, where she was. *"Sorry. I can't focus well,"* she said as he seemed to flood her mind.

Red rage blossomed in his mind as he took inventory. The injuries were minor, for now. *"He's gone. He doesn't think I'll wake up for a little while,"* she told him silently as he counted each bruise. So far, all of them had been acquired during her abduction. Bruises from the long ride there in the trunk, abrasions on her wrists from the rope, a slap across her face when she had turned to face him in the kitchen of her apartment that morning. She had glimpsed his face, had felt his mind.

"Who in the fuck is it?" he demanded as he continued to work his way over her body. He jerked when his lips actually moved and was startled to realize he was actually alone in the room. The link was so complete he had forgotten, for a brief moment, she wasn't there with him.

"Colton. It's Colton. And it's not me he's focused on. It's my mother…he's been kidnapping my mother. He was obsessed with her."

"Be quiet," he said gruffly. "Where are you?"

"I don't know. But I think I can bring you to me. Just follow me." He felt the shadow of a smile on her face, the pain it caused to arc through her head, and he cursed furiously. *"I'll be your compass. We're bound together. That's why I felt so safe when you came back and I just now figured it out. You'll find me. We don't need the transmitter or anything else. Just each other. Find me, Seth."*

His car was still in the shop. So he did the practical thing. He stole the first car he came upon. It was a knack a lot of cops had, but he had learned it even earlier. His mama had an iron fist, but he had slipped out of it from time to time, and had run wild in the streets. Hotwiring a car was child's play. Following that odd lingering feel in the air that was Erin was even easier. He hit the highway and headed east to the lake

* * * * *

She was strapped to the floor, with each wrist to a chained ring and each ankle bound as well by leather cuffs with heavy metal links, locked to more rings. A drain was to her right and she shuddered as she eyed it. Such a familiar picture.

The drain was to wash her blood away.

He'd pour bleach down it. And sulphuric acid. Nothing ever truly dissolved human blood but it was enough to wash away her DNA and keep them from linking her disappearance to him. Assuming anybody linked him to the crimes.

He wasn't bargaining on Seth.

Of course, he wasn't going to leave here alive.

But he was finished, either way.

"You're awake."

The voice wasn't the low menacing one it had been for the others. She rolled her head to the side and said, "Decide to stop playacting, Chief?" Her arms were stretched so tightly overhead it hurt, but she refused to show she was even uncomfortable. She had managed to lose the earring in the trunk, as Seth had told her, just by rubbing her head on her shoulder. Both of them were in there now. She hadn't been able to locate either one by feel, so had been relieved when she had been able to reach out and touch Seth's mind so completely.

"You're so like your mother, Erin. Ever the lady," Colton said, moving out of the shadows. "It was playacting. All to pique your curiosity, this time around, at least. I had intended to take her, but your dumbfuck father killed her."

"And for that I will thank him every day for the rest of my life," Erin said with heartfelt sincerity. That heartbreaking accident that had taken her mama and daddy had been a gift, and she had just now realized it. "And if I die today, or tomorrow, or the next day, my first stop is going to be to thank God for the car crash, for keeping her from you. I've always known things happen for a reason, and this is the reason she died when she did, to be kept away from something as awful as you."

"She should have been mine," Colton hissed, moving closer, his small eyes ugly, angry and enraged. "Your slobbering, blue-collar father didn't deserve her. She was a Vincent, one of the blue bloods. Her family is as old as mine and—"

"And her first dog was better looking than you?" Erin supplied helpfully.

She saw the confusion in his eyes, then the rage. She watched as he raised his hand and then she closed her eyes and willed herself not to feel it. She wasn't going to fight him yet. He had loved it when they fought back, and she wasn't going to give that to him yet. She blanked her mind and then she felt Seth reaching for her.

And she had to block him as well when the first blow fell open-handed across her face.

Seth felt her cut him off and he wanted to howl.

He sped down the gravel road, following her. It felt as though there was a thread drawing him closer and closer, and the closer he got, the tighter the thread became.

"Erin," he growled, reaching for her. "Erin, damn it, let me in."

"No. Not now. You're close, I can feel it. I'll be okay until then."

And then she was gone again.

She opened her eyes, licked the blood away from her mouth and glared up at Colton. Then she narrowed her eyes as he started to jerk his clothes open and away. "Big mistake, Chief. As long I didn't figure you were ready to start with the rape, I could handle the beating," she drawled, focusing her mind.

He had just turned his small pig-like eyes back to her, opening his mouth to hiss at her again when she struck. His scream bounced off the walls, echoing as she struck again.

He drew his knife, one hand held to his head, hardly able to see beyond the pain. The knife was flashing down, just like she had seen. She felt it slash her thigh and she lashed out again with her mind, harder and stronger. In his rage, he was able to strike back, even though she ripped something open inside his brain, causing him to bleed.

This time he moved higher and had better aim, striking her belly, cutting her shallowly, but enough to make her bleed. *If Seth didn't get here soon* — she pushed the thought aside, shoved the pain aside, and struck out. The knife was descending and she didn't even realize how different this was from her visions. The rape hadn't happened, she knew help was coming.

The door banged open, a howl filled the air, and Erin felt the terror leave her and she sagged back against the floor. She decided then it was fairly safe to pass out, and she conceded to the beckoning black waves with gratitude. She'd be sorry later — she hadn't lost that much blood. But enough that the fear made oblivion seem fairly sweet.

Seth took Colton to the ground, snapping his arm. Blood was pouring from his eyes, ears, nose and even his mouth. Massive brain hemorrhage, Seth was figuring, but the fury and insanity there were masking the pain. Seth's own insanity more than made them an even pair though, as Seth held him down and Colton fought to get back to killing Erin.

"That's my woman you marked," he breathed into Colton's ear, drawing his gun, pressing the cold metal to Colton's neck. One arm broken, the other shoved high and twisted behind his back, he could only fight so hard, and the injury inside his head was slowly killing him. "My woman you tried to kill. I'd see you dead for it, but she's already started the job. It'd be my pleasure to stay and watch it finished, but I've a need to see her to the hospital now."

"Mine..." Colton hissed.

"Mine," Seth said. "Know why she was just now available for you to grab? Were you able to hear inside her apartment? No? I've been with her, every night, loving that long sweet, body."

"Mine..." the voice was weaker. But he glared at Seth with furious, hate-filled eyes as Seth got up and stood over him, his lip curled in disgust as Colton tried to climb to his feet. But he was already too weak. Too unfocused.

Slowly, he backed away and went to Erin. The heavily padlocked leather cuffs held her chained like something less than an animal. The bleeding mess of a man lying on the floor, breathing in shallow pants, hadn't paid enough. But Erin bled as well, from numerous thin slices that marred her pale, lovely body.

Her eyes remained closed as he checked frantically for a pulse. It pounded steadily, and her skin was warm and smooth, her chest moving steadily up and down.

A harsh gurgling noise came from Colton's mouth as Seth pulled his lock picks from his pocket. Sliding him a glance, Seth started working the locks. "She'll die with...me. I made...sure of...it," Colton hissed.

"No, you didn't," Seth said flatly. "She was smarter than you. Instead of getting pissed and losing her cool like you did, she fought. You fucking coward. Tied down and helpless and she could still fight braver than you could. They are waiting for you in hell."

Colton started to laugh as Seth freed the second wrist. "I'm taking her with me," he insisted, rolling onto his side and lifting his gun.

A shot filled the room before Seth could even drop the lock pick. Flinging his body across Erin's, he waited for the pain that would fill him, but it never came.

"Sorry bastard. They'll lock the gate behind that one in hell, that's for sure," a wry, tired voice muttered.

Slowly, Seth lifted his eyes and met Eddie's across the room.

"You know, it's a funny thing being a partner. You're actually expected to notify your partner when you are in need of backup. But you young punks probably have a hard time remembering that," Eddie said, smirking a bit as he pulled his jacket off and offered it to Seth.

"I'll...ah...I'll remember that."

"Good luck, Eddie. His head is harder than a rock," a soft, muffled voice murmured.

Slowly, he rose and stared down into dazed, glassy eyes. "Erin," he rasped, tossing the jacket over her before he caught her under the arms and lifted her up, gently cradling her against him.

"Careful there, bud. She's still pinned at the legs," Eddie murmured. "But you just hold tight. I think she needs that right now."

"Yeah," she whispered. "Hold tight—I do need it."

"I need it, too." Seth pressed his cheek against her hair and rocked her gently as the sound of sirens in the distance grew louder.

Epilogue

CHIEF OF POLICE GUILTY OF MURDER?
DEAD BY MYSTERIOUS MASSIVE BRAIN HEMORRHAGE

Erin glanced up from her hospital bed where she was reading the newspaper headlines to look at Seth. "Do I really have to read this?"

He shrugged. "I wasn't sure if you wanted to or not," he said. "Did you notice the date?" he asked.

She lifted a blonde brow. "I do know my own birthday," she said with a smile.

"Good." The door opened and a nurse wheeled in a cake, balloons and flowers. After she had left, Seth lowered himself to the chair and stared at her over the back. "We're having a party, a big one, after you come home and are feeling up to it. But I wanted this quiet. Because I wanted to give you this."

She stared at the dark blue jeweler's box with misty eyes, hardly able to breathe as he opened it. When he slid the ring on her hand, he said, "You told me you'd say yes, so do I have to ask, or can we just set a date?"

She laughed through the tears and said, "How does *now* sound?"

THE EMPATH'S LOVER

Chapter One

Jordan slammed the phone down. Her back hurt, her arches ached, her head was pounding, and her suitcases were on their way to Toledo.

This was not the way she had intended to start her vacation. She had actually wrapped up her trip to Williamsburg a week early, and had returned to Indianapolis on an evening flight without calling Lee, but if she had known the fucking problems she would have…

She sighed and shoved her hair out of her eyes. The choppy black bangs fell right back into her eyes again and she suppressed the urge to scream with rage. It was a bad hair day, on top of everything else.

She punched another number into the phone. She could probably get hold of Kaitlyn, her assistant manager. But nooo…

Kaitlyn wasn't answering her home phone or the pager after thirty minutes. Jordan was about to call for a cab, reaching into her purse to find a credit card. She had no ready cash on hand, but plastic worked. A card fell out of her wallet and fluttered to the nubby teal carpet and she knelt, picking it up, rubbing her thumb over the print.

Angelo Investigations, Inc.

She knew the number by heart.

Angelo was Lee's twin brother. He was going to be Lee's best man at their wedding in eight weeks. They talked on occasion, ran into each other rarely. No reason to know the number by heart.

But she did.

Jordan didn't really like Angelo. It was short for Michelangelo, of all things. And Lee was short, yep, for Leonardo. Neither of the men would acknowledge what their mom was thinking when she named them.

Angelo was too...*there*. Everything about him was too alive—his eyes, his voice, his hands, the way he talked and moved.

The way he made her feel. He looked at her and she felt like she had touched a live wire.

It was odd—he and Lee were identical twins. But only Angelo made her feel like that. He was just too *much*.

Yeah, too much.

She scraped her blood-red thumbnail over the embossed number and whispered, "The hell with it. I'm tired."

She dialed the number and insisted it was not sexual heat she felt when he answered the phone moments later with a gruff, "Angelo."

* * * * *

Angelo rolled onto his back and laid the phone in the cradle, lying there briefly and pondering the phone call before jackknifing out of bed.

Hot damn.

Jordan Sears. His brother's pretty little faerie, with her big green eyes and spiky black hair...he should feel guilty over how excited just hearing her voice made him. And a few weeks ago he would have—hell, he had. He had avoided his favorite bookstore, which she owned, so he wouldn't run into her. He avoided his brother outside of work so he wouldn't see her.

But now — hot damn.

He didn't know why he didn't do so now, but Angelo had learned long ago not to question his instincts. He made his living off them.

He jerked his jeans over his naked hips, thankful he had at least managed to get some clothes clean before falling into a stupor early this morning. He had spent the last week tracking a kid whose dad had decided to skip town with him. If the dad hadn't been sliding the boy downers to keep him quiet and malleable, it wouldn't have taken so long. But the boy's emotions were repressed, abnormal, and it had taken a little longer than Angelo had expected.

Now they just had to get the drugs out of his system. He was sleeping it off in the hospital, and his bastard of a father was in the downtown jail. Probably wouldn't stay, he thought, as he jerked a T-shirt on and jammed his feet into boots.

Angelo was a touch empath.

He could touch an object a person had held and know their fears, their thoughts, their needs. He could hold something of personal value and use it to lock in on that person, eventually. It made his job easier and harder, trying to explain to the cops how he had just followed a lead...

He was out the door in five minutes. And he didn't bother with the car, even though Jordan was bound to have luggage. He threw one long jeans-clad leg over the Harley, made sure he had the extra helmet. There was always an extra jacket stowed. A few minutes later he was on I-65 and heading towards Indianapolis International, a hot grin on his face.

He didn't know where in the fuck Lee was.

And he didn't care.

He was going to see Jordan.

He would get to touch her.

She belonged to his brother, she would be marrying his brother, and Angelo respected that. Hell, he was probably going to have to leave town just to keep his distance. She didn't like him, and that made it easier, but damn it…he wanted her so bad.

He had started falling just a little in love with her from the first, when she had slid out of the car while Lee continued to sit inside, talking business on his cell phone, yakking away while his pretty little faerie stared at Angelo with wide, nervous eyes. Her first thought of Angelo was one that wouldn't ever leave him…*I'd never mistake him for Lee…*

Of course, it had felt like an insult.

But Angelo knew too many things about Lee. Broken dinner dates, late business meetings that really weren't that important—Lee didn't seem to realize what a prize he had in Jordan.

He took the turnoff for the airport and felt his body tighten in anticipation. The bike's engine sounded twice as loud under the sheltering overhang provided for the people waiting for their rides.

The thriving masses, so many different moods.

Anger, frustration, happiness, sadness, loneliness— the airport was a living, breathing thing to Angelo's senses. His shields fell into place almost automatically, and he hated that he had to keep them in place as he saw Jordan pacing the sidewalk. He wanted to know what she was thinking, feeling, dreaming.

She had said curtly, "I'll wait out front. Thanks, Angelo."

He slowed the bike to a stop as he caught sight of her and pulled his helmet off, waiting until she looked his way.

Her eyes widened and she stopped in her tracks. And even with his shielding in place, he could feel her surprise. "You want me to ride on the Harley," she said, her voice oddly...rough?

Her short, spiky black hair looked more tousled than normal as she moved a little closer. "I'm sorry," he lied easily. "I wasn't even thinking about your bags."

She scowled, her rosebud mouth puckering. "Don't have any," she sulked. "They are en route to Toledo." She slid him a look that warned him not to laugh.

He smiled. "Bad day, Jordan?" he asked.

"The worst," she sighed. She slid her eyes back to the bike. "I...how am I supposed to ride that without touching you, Angelo?"

He grinned. "I don't know exactly what Lee's told you, Jordan. But I've got no problems having a pretty woman touching me. I can pretty much pick and choose what I want to absorb. And unless it's skin to skin contact, there's not much I'll pick up." *Liar.* Angelo's gifts had started out that he had to be in direct contact, back when he was five or six. But the older he got, just close proximity could do it.

And now…it didn't even have to be very close proximity. He could drop his shields and be overcome by the emotions of nearly every person waiting out here, and quite a few of the people in the immediate area inside.

So when she climbed on, unless he decided to shield good and tight, he would know damn good and well what she was feeling.

But she didn't have to know that. Hell, even Lee didn't know exactly how refined Angelo's gifts had become over the past decade, especially the past few years.

She hesitated and Angelo rolled his eyes. "C'mon, or do you want to wait here all night for Lee? Look, I can touch you and be just fine." He reached up and laid both hands on her cheeks, staring down into her big green eyes, maintaining his indifferent face, grinning almost absently all the while.

But–*hot damn*–the emotions inside her…

Exhaustion, yearning, hunger, loneliness, frustration, aching, burning needs that he wondered if his brother was even *aware* of. Lee treated Jordan like she was made of spun glass. He pulled his hands away a hell of a lot quicker than he wanted to—he had found something he hadn't expected to find. Jordan didn't dislike him.

She wanted him.

He made her nervous.

She was afraid of him.

Afraid of…how *alive?* What a weird way to put it.

Thoughtfully, he smoothed a hand over the back of her tense neck and urged her toward the bike. And discovered something else new.

Hot little licks of frustrated longing…all centered around a big black Harley. Angelo couldn't help the grin that split his face as he pulled the spare jacket out. Damn it, what in the hell was he going to do about this?

*****

As Angelo helped with the helmet, to distract herself, she asked, "Do you know where Lee is? I've been trying to get hold of him for a couple of hours."

He shrugged. "I haven't talked to him much this week. Bad week. Busy," he said. His eyes—dark brown, like Lee's, but they seemed so much warmer and softer—drifted down to meet Jordan's before he lowered the visor. "If he had known you were coming, he'd be home."

"I know," she muttered, shifting on the seat. *A Harley. I'm sitting on a Harley. With Angelo Kelley.* Too fucking bad it wasn't Lee. Then she frowned. Something told her Angelo was the better of the twins to spend time on a Harley with. She glanced up, caught an odd glitter in his eyes, almost like he knew what she was thinking.

No. He didn't. He didn't have Lee's unusual skills. His were all about the feelings, and he had to be touching. And he hadn't been touching her. Lee could catch random thoughts, hear them, but not Angelo. *Damn good thing Lee wasn't around right now,* she thought darkly.

Angelo turned away, but not before she caught sight of a grin on his lean, tanned face. His longish blond hair was still in a stubby ponytail and he slid his helmet on before mounting the bike easily, even though he had gotten her on first, shown her how to sit, made sure she was comfortable.

Not, her mind shrieked. The bike roared to life and Jordan shuddered as her entire body did the same.

Damn it, it was more than she had thought.

"Hold on," Angelo told her, shouting over the rumble of the engine. She leaned forward, tentatively wrapping her arms around his waist. "Tighter, Jordan." She was trusting him here and hoping that the leather separating them was going to do what Angelo had insinuated— hoping he did have to have skin-to-skin contact—because if he didn't, she'd never be able to look at him again.

Jordan's fantasy in life was to get swept away by a big, brawny, sexy biker, taken away somewhere, given no choice or say in it while that big, sexy man had his way with her and fucked her six different ways to Sunday. And Angelo definitely fit the bill, six-foot-four, sun-streaked golden hair, melted-chocolate eyes, big shoulders, big muscled arms, wide muscled chest...

*Oh, damn...*she was getting wet. Her nipples stabbed into the lace of her bra and she squirmed uncomfortably, then wished she hadn't as the friction stimulated her clit and brought a gasp to her lips.

A deep, shuddering sort of sigh rippled through Angelo but she hardly noticed as she unconsciously shifted a little closer while he wove in and out of traffic. The house she shared with Lee was about forty minutes away...damn it, she wasn't going to be able to handle this.

Damn it, he couldn't handle this.

Her thighs cradled him and she had shifted forward so that she was pressed tightly against him, as tightly as she could be with the layers of clothing between them. He shouldn't have let his guard down when he touched her.

But how in the fuck was he to know how strongly she was drawn to him? Or the kinds of fantasies she had lurking in her mind? His cock throbbed under his jeans as he headed back down I-65 south. She wasn't even aware of it, but she was rocking against him...fuck!

He hoped like hell Lee was home.

Otherwise he was going to have a fight with himself to keep from touching her. If he was a nice brother, an honorable brother, he would call Lee. They had a link, most twins had some type, but theirs was a special one. And Jordan was wrong. Angelo's gifts went above even what Lee knew about.

But Angelo didn't call out to Lee. He didn't want his brother picking up on his emotional state, or his physical one.

His breath hissed out between his teeth when her hands slid down from his waist down, her hand absently brushing over his cock as she shifted her grip from his waist to his hips, while she continued to unconsciously rock her pelvis against him.

Chapter Two

Jordan could hardly breathe. The helmet wasn't helping, but that wasn't the problem. The problem was this damn bike—it was like a giant vibrator. And the problem was Angelo. It was his fault. She was feeling guilty, too. He was big and sexy and he looked like the man she loved, and he had put her on this giant vibrator. He had put her on her fantasy, and how in the hell was she going to explain this to Lee?

She squirmed a little more and hoped like hell he was home.

Otherwise, she was going to have one long, frustrating night.

Then she started hoping he wasn't. If he wasn't she could pull out her own vibrator, handle the problem that way and forget this little episode. With her luck he'd give her the sexual equivalent of a pat on the head, some nice sweet missionary sex, which she was *really* starting to hate, a sweet little kiss on the lips, then cuddle her into sleep, and she'd still be wanting a good hard fuck—damn it!

It was Angelo's fault, she thought, sulking, shifting and squirming on the leather, rocking against his firm ass absently, reveling in his rather unique scent while the wind whipped past them as he took the exit to her house.

Lee was home all right.

She climbed off, stood there on weak, shaky knees, felt Angelo slide one hand under her arm as he guided her up to the porch. She shouldn't have needed help, but she had been lingering on the verge of orgasm for forty-five fucking minutes — damn it, she hoped Lee didn't pick up on that.

Angelo lashed his shields down tightly. He didn't want Lee picking up anything from him right now. He wished he could do the same with Jordan but there wasn't any help for that. She was about five seconds away from having an orgasm, and Angelo would have given his right arm, his kidney, and his empathy just to be the one to give her that orgasm.

But, no, she belonged to Lee.

And Lee was going to have the fucking pleasure, again.

With a humorless smile, he took her keys from her shaking hands and opened the door, guiding her inside the house.

Lee had heard his bike.

His brother was shouting from the other end of the sprawling house. "Angelo, get the fuck out — "

Jordan stood frozen, her flushed face slowly going pale, her head cocked to the side as she studied the room before her. Her big, green eyes looked black in her face. She stood staring at a beaded blue cocktail gown and a woman's purse lying on the floor. A little further away, one shoe, and then the other, and as she stood there with Angelo's hand under her arm, staring, she heard a woman's laugh, followed by a moan, and the unmistakable sounds of sex.

"No, Jordan," Angelo whispered gruffly, tugging her back towards the door.

"Angelo," she said quietly, pulling her elbow away.

She walked soundlessly down the hall, following the sounds of moaning, and heard a hand striking flesh. She stopped and shuddered. Lee treated her like an antique, a lady, a flower in bed. Oh, he was a good lover, but he was also a gentleman. God forbid he should spank her while he fucked her.

She felt Angelo at her back.

"Angelo, I told you to get the fuck out. This doesn't—oh, damn it, do that again—concern you," Lee shouted.

The shouting wasn't necessary. They stood in the doorway, watching as Lee drove his cock into the ass of a ripe redhead. Tears stung Jordan's eyes. She knew that woman. It was Kaitlyn. As she watched, Lee spanked her again and Kaitlyn moaned and said, "Do it again, damn it. Fuck me harder, Lee. Damn it, I love it."

Lee drove harder into her and a tiny, distressed sound left Jordan's mouth. It was drowned out by Lee snapping, still unaware of her, "I didn't know you were so into watching, bro. Kait, you want a double fuck? You can lose Jordan's vibrator and we could—"

Angelo heard her though. Wrapping one strong arm around her waist, he whispered, "Shh, honey." He drew her back against him, rubbing her arm gently, nuzzling her crown with his chin, his gentle concern masking the rage he felt. "Such loyalty you two motherfuckers have," he said casually, the ice dripping off his voice catching the attention of the pair on the bed.

"Lee's right," Jordan said huskily as the pair on the bed finally froze and noticed *she* was standing there. "This doesn't concern you, I guess. But it does concern me." She twisted the ring off her finger and dropped it on the floor.

Shifting gently out of Angelo's supportive embrace she turned and walked on shaking legs down the hall and out of the house.

"Jordan," Lee rasped, his face going red.

Kaitlyn's mouth moved but no sound came out.

Angelo lifted a brow at them. Lee surged off the bed, shouting Jordan's name but Angelo blocked the door and laid a hand on his brother's bare shoulder, narrowing his eyes as he absorbed. "You fucking bastard," he whispered. "Her money? Is that all that mattered to you?"

"Not all, no," Lee snarled. "Get the fuck out of my way."

Kaitlyn clambered down off the bed. "Angelo, Lee cares about Jordan. This is my fault—"

They all heard the door slam.

Angelo smirked. "I don't care whose fault it is. She's not going to forget what she just saw. And I'm going to make damn sure of that," he drawled. He cocked his head at his brother. "I've got something I oughta share with you, bro. I've been in love with your *ex*-fiancée for months. So maybe I should say thank you to both of you."

Lee lunged at him but Angelo had already moved away.

He caught up with Jordan as she stood staring at her keys with blank eyes. Her fire-engine-red BMW was in the drive and she was staring at the keys, then at the car like she didn't know what in the fuck she was supposed to do.

"C'mon," Angelo said gruffly, taking her keys and pocketing them. "Lee's going to come looking for you. You go off by yourself and he'll find you. You want that?"

"No," she whispered soundlessly.

It had always been so romantic, Lee being able to find her without half trying…but the thought of seeing him now, she suppressed a shudder. "Did you know?"

"No," he said quietly, leading her back to the bike and just lifting her up and putting her on it. He put the helmet on her and mounted. Lee was opening the door and running out, still jerking his pants up.

Right as they pulled out of the drive, Lee got to them. Angelo flipped his brother off as Lee was reaching out to Jordan, looking properly anguished. Jordan turned her head away from him, thanking the helmet that muffled his voice.

She rode in a daze. It was getting cooler. Several hours had passed. Her thighs were aching, her tail was sore from spending so much time on the bike. But her mind…she had succeeded in blissfully blanking her mind.

She lifted her head only when the rumbling stopped. Looking around, she realized they were in a clearing, a little log cabin in front of them, water glinting off a lake behind them. "Where are we?" she asked hoarsely.

"My cabin," Angelo said. "You need a place to let your thoughts settle, I reckon."

"Do you know how long it's been going on?" she asked.

He threw a leg over the front of the bike and turned to face her, studying her in the moonlight. Gently, he took the helmet off and looped it over a handlebar. He ran his fingers through her hair, settled them at her neck and massaged. "A while. Now's not the time to talk about this, Jordan. You're too hurt," he said softly. "It's been going on a while. I didn't know. I would have told you if I had."

Solemnly, blinking her eyes at him owl-like, she said, "You read him?"

"Yeah."

"There's more to it, isn't there?"

"Afraid so," he replied, digging his fingers a little more firmly into her supple skin. "I can't believe that jackass is my blood."

"It's not gonna work, saying he's the milkman's boy. The resemblance is too strong" she told him, smirking a little, looking a little more like the feisty Jordan he knew, a little less lost. "Kaitlyn...she's my best friend. Was," she whispered.

"Stop thinking about it," he whispered. He leaned down, cursing himself, but knowing it was for the best. Catching her eyes with his, he waited until she was staring at him and he focused, then he pulled her under.

She slumped forward, asleep.

He took her from the bike, carrying her inside the cabin. He lay down with her on the bed, wrapping his big body around her smaller one and whispered into her ear, "You're mine, Jordan. I'm sorry he hurt you, but I'm glad it happened. Because now I can have you, and I'm going to keep you."

You're mine, Jordan. I'm sorry he hurt you, but I'm glad it happened. Because now I can have you, and I'm going to keep you.

Jordan heard the rumbled words distantly in her sleep, and wondered if she was dreaming.

There was something else hovering at the edge of her consciousness, something awful, that she didn't want to think about. She shied away from it, and burrowed into the warm presence that curled around her, shutting whatever that awful thing was away.

That's it, baby. You don't have to think about it. She sighed, rolled over. Rubbed her cheek against a broad, warm chest. *Lee?* She wondered absently. Then she shuddered. Not Lee. Lee had done something…he was what she didn't want think about.

No. It's not Lee. Sleep, Jordan. Just sleep, baby.

With a sigh, she slid deeper into sleep and shuddered as a big, broad hand stroked down her back and settled on her hip, pulling her lower body closer to the wonderful source of heat.

He was right. There was nothing really worth thinking about, was there?

No. Nothing at all.

Chapter Three

Even in her sleep, she had realized it wasn't Lee holding her. Angelo was trying hard not to be too satisfied with that as he slid from the bed. He laid a hand on her brow and told himself he was just doing it for her own good as he made sure she wasn't going to wake up too soon.

She seriously did need to sleep.

About ten years ago Angelo had developed a new talent, something connected to his empathy, something that allowed him to do what he had done to Jordan earlier. Just guided her into sleep. He had used it to hypnotize others before, a few times. He used it rarely because he was uncomfortable with it. People shouldn't have gifts that could allow them to coerce others.

And if Jordan hadn't been through what she had been through today...

Damn it, he *really* wanted ten minutes alone with Lee. Just ten fucking minutes. How in the fuck—

He felt the pressure on his mind and left the room before he acknowledged it. It was Lee, looking for him. The touch was like a knocking on the inside of his mind. Angelo could have ignored him but there was no point. Yet.

What in the fuck do you want?

Where in the hell are you? Where's Jordan? Lee demanded.

None of your business, bro. She gave you your ring back, remember?

That's for me and her to discuss. Bring her back. Otherwise, I'll find her.

Angelo smirked and flopped down on his couch, staring out the window into the darkness of the night. *You can always try.*

He felt the presence of Lee's reach as he probed and he felt Lee's surprise as he easily deflected it. *Surprise, big brother,* Angelo said, laughing out loud. *If you had bothered to keep in touch, you might have realized little brother has been discovering some new tricks.*

Jordan is mine, Lee said flatly. Lee's mental voice was as clear to Angelo as though he was standing in the room. When he chose, he could even make others without the talent hear it. But Lee hadn't realized that somewhere along the line, Angelo had picked up those same gifts. And Lee hadn't developed any new talents at all.

You don't love her, Lee. You hurt her. Even if she never found out, you still hurt her. Kait was her best friend and you two betrayed her. It's unforgivable. If you loved her, it wouldn't have happened.

Stay out of this, Angelo. You just want her because she's mine, Lee warned.

Wrong, Angelo said quietly. He opened his eyes and thought of Jordan, sleeping in his sprawling bed under the skylight, her eyes still swollen from the tears she had cried on the ride up here. *She cried, Lee. For hours. You hurt her, and you don't really care about anything except losing what she can do for you. She's not yours.*

She's mine now, and I'm keeping her, Angelo said softly. Then he dropped his shields back in place, closing Lee off, easily and quickly. And none of the pounding Lee subjected him to could change that. He checked on Jordan, made sure she was still sleeping before he headed out.

They needed food.

He needed a few other things. He was going to mark his claim on her tonight...and what better way to do it than by giving her the fantasies he had seen lurking in her mind?

Jordan awoke to the feel of Angelo sleeping at her back. A large, warm, oddly comforting presence. She squeezed her eyes closed against the memory of yesterday, and wished she had stayed in Williamsburg a few more days.

But then she might not have found out for a long time.

Maybe never.

"Go back to sleep," Angelo whispered against her ear, his voice low and rough.

"I've slept enough," she said hoarsely. "It's not going to undo it."

"Hmmm. Guess not," he murmured. She shuddered as he buried his face against her neck and breathed in deeply. The arm he had banded around her waist tightened. Jordan felt liquid heat pool in her belly, felt her sex clench. Against her butt, she felt the hard, firm length of Angelo's cock. "You smell so sweet, Jordan."

"Angelo..."

"I've spent the past year hating my brother for having you," he whispered, raking her neck with his teeth and rocking his cock into her, flattening his hand against her belly and holding her still. "If I had any idea he would have treated you like this…"

Jordan's breath caught in her throat as the hand that had been resting rather innocently on her belly slid up and cupped her breast. "I wanted you the first time I saw you, Jordan. You belonged to my brother and I couldn't have you," he told her as he rolled her nipple between his thumb and forefinger. "Will you let me now?"

No. That was what she should have said. But she was frozen and unable to answer as he rolled her onto her back and covered her mouth with his, driving his tongue deep inside to taunt and torment her while his hands went to the buttons on her shirt. His hands cupped her breasts as he ate at her mouth, hungrily, avidly. Jordan gasped as he pinched her nipples through her bra, causing them to bead up into tight, stiff points.

His mouth left hers to close over one nipple, sucking roughly through the lace. Jerking it down, the lace pressed against her breast, framing it, the aureole red and tight from his touch. "Will you, Jordan? I want you, want to taste you, touch you, fuck you. You want it, don't you? Lee treated you like a lady, didn't he? You want to be treated like a woman, not a doll," he murmured as he licked and nuzzled her breast, then moved across and shoved the lace down from her other breast.

Lifting up, he studied her, the lace from her underwire bra pushed down, framing her breasts, pushing them higher. "That's pretty," he decided, then he lifted his chocolate eyes and studied her green ones. "I know what you want, what you dream about. I can give you that and more," he whispered, bending low to catch one plump nipple and bite down hard enough, just this side of pain, watching as her lashes lifted, then fluttered down, while her back arched up and a shudder racked her long, slender body.

She cried out as he slid his hand inside her loose-fitting, wide-legged black trousers, inside the black lace thong she wore, and pressed his fingers against her clit, rubbing it with slow, maddening strokes. She sobbed his name as he pushed two long, thick fingers inside her tight, wet vagina, quick and hard. Jordan closed her hands into his long, golden-blond hair, holding him tight against her.

"Say yes, think yes, and I'll know," he told her as he fucked her with his fingers, moving higher on her body and staring into her eyes. "I'll show you things my brother would never dream of doing to you. He has this idea about how to treat you—and I know it doesn't mesh with what you want, does it?"

Mutely, she shook her head.

Beguiling, he whispered, "Tell me yes, think it, and I'll make you feel more loved and needed than you've ever felt in your life, Jordan."

"Yes," she whimpered, then she screamed, "*Please!*" as he thrust his fingers high and hard, bringing her to quick and sudden climax. The muscles in her pussy clamped down on his fingers and she lifted up against him, riding it, rocking against him and clutching at his big, wide shoulders while she arched up and kissed him hungrily.

Jordan was still a bit dazed when she felt him stretching her arms overhead. It was the cool snick of metal against her wrists that woke her out of her daze, she decided. If it wasn't for the hungry, *tender* look in Angelo's eyes, she might have been scared witless.

But as he reached underneath her, grasping the neck of her shirt, all she could think was…

Oh, man…

She felt the shirt fall away from her shoulders with a loud, abrupt rip. He smiled, a slow, wolfish smile, as he ran his thumb along the edge of the scalloped lace of her bra. "It looks pretty, framing your breasts like that. We can leave it. And your pants won't be so much trouble." And they weren't. He slid them off, quick and easy as you please, sliding the flats of his hands down her legs, slowly caressing them with a slow, downward stroke as he stripped the article of clothing away, leaving her black lace thong in place.

"And that's pretty, too," he mused, brushing the back of his fingers against it. "Let's have a taste."

She cried out when he grabbed her thighs, spread them wide and pressed his face against the lace, stabbing his tongue against it, sucking at her clit greedily, until she was rocking up against him. He jerked the lace out of the way, used two fingers to part the lips of her sex, and speared her with his tongue, groaning as her taste flooded his mouth. Jordan flexed her wrists against the cuffs that held her hands pinned, sobbing when he moved higher, fastening his mouth on her clit and suckling, then working two fingers back inside her slippery wet pussy.

She made a soft, forlorn sound low in her throat when he pulled away, and he laughed, pressing kisses to her navel, her torso, her nipples, her neck as he moved up her body. When he kissed her, deep and rough, she tasted herself on him, and blushed, trying to pull away. "Mmmm, no, baby. Can't have that," he murmured, holding her face still with one hand. He pulled his fingers from the tight grip of her pussy and used them to paint her cream onto her lips, watching as blood stained her cheeks red. "Dessert," he crooned. "My favorite." Then he captured her face with his hands and caught her mouth roughly with his. Kissing her voraciously, groaning deep and low in his chest, he plunged his tongue deep, and thrust his jeans-covered cock against the softness of her belly.

She shuddered as he released her face long enough to jerk at the opening of his jeans, freeing his cock. She felt it burning into her belly, hard as rock, silky smooth, hotter than a branding iron. A soft gentle brush *inside* her head. *When Lee made love to you, did he use a rubber?* Angelo purred as he took her mouth again, kissing her deeply while he forced his thoughts into her head.

Only...Lee had told her Angelo couldn't do that.

Lee doesn't know me as well as he thinks. Answer me. When he touched you, when he fucked you, did he wear a rubber?

Yes, she thought as disgust and shame rolled through her. He had been her only lover, and she hadn't thought it was necessary. She was on the pill for crying out loud, and she hated the smell, the feel of latex. Lee had told her they needed the extra protection.

Maybe you did, Angelo whispered inside her mind. *But we don't.*

Whimpering low in her throat, she rocked against him, squirmed and wriggled, dying to feel him inside, feel him fuck her hard —

A loud scream escaped her as he did just that, using his thighs to spread hers wide and taking his cock in hand, aiming for her entrance and driving in to the hilt with one long, ruthless thrust that stole her breath. Burning, tearing pressure arced through her as molten pleasure flooded her groin and spilled outward. Jordan's heart started to pound with slow, thrumming beats that echoed in her womb as he pulled out and surged back inside, lifting his head and staring down into her eyes as he joined his naked flesh to hers.

"You don't have any idea how long, how badly I've wanted to do this," he muttered, reaching up and unlocking one of the cuffs, so that her hands came free. Pinning her wrists with one of his hands, he held her down as he started to thrust deep and hard, shuddering at the wet, clinging clasp of her pussy on his cock. "Every damn time...I thought of Lee...touching you like this..."

"He never did," she whimpered, arching her hips, trying to hold him inside as he pulled out. "Not like this."

He smiled, a sexy, lopsided curl of his mouth that heated her insides even more. "Never made you feel like I will," he promised hotly, as he released her wrists and rose to his knees, catching her thighs and opening her legs wide, draping them over his forearms and staring down at the display she made, her labia spread wide around the thickness of his cock, her clit hard, gleaming and swollen.

Pushing slowly back inside her, he whispered, "Play with yourself, Jordan. Show me how you like to be touched. So I can do it later."

The blood rose again to her cheeks as she slowly slid one of her freed hands down, the cuff still dangling from her wrist as she stroked her clit in slow, hesitant circles. He cocked a brow at her, his blond hair spilling into his dark eyes. "Is that really how you like it?" he asked doubtfully as he drove his cock high and hard inside her, bringing a gasp to her lips.

She arched up, lifting her breasts, a moan falling from her as the pleasure streaked through her in hot, fast licks.

Quickly, she circled her fingers around her clit, falling into a familiar rhythm. "That's better," he purred in praise, hunkering over her and settling into a deep, driving rhythm that had his large muscled body shuddering, his balls drawing taut against his body. Her tight, narrow little vagina hugged him snugly, her slender torso heaving as she panted for air, her rounded little breasts topped with tightly drawn nipples, red and peaked.

Her slim fingers started to gleam from her cream as she stroked her clit, her lids drooping, her head arching back while she hummed in her throat. "Damn..." she sighed, her tongue sliding out to wet her lips. An orgasm was starting to build. She could feel it. And it was gonna be massive...every muscle in her body was starting to tighten, the muscles in her thighs quivering as he held them splayed with his big hands. The thick head of his cock rasped over the rich bed of nerves buried at the mouth of her womb, once, twice, then a third time, as she lightly scraped her nails over her clit. Jordan's back arched up and she went screaming into orgasm, the muscles in her sheath locking down and convulsing on his cock.

He groaned, sounding like he was in agony, and slammed into her repeatedly, his large body crushing down on her, trapping her hand between them. He took her mouth savagely, hungrily, driving his tongue inside and stealing her breath. His thoughts barreled into her brain and she trembled, overwhelmed by the force of the orgasm ripping through her, by the force of his need and emotions...*tight wet, love you sweet...damn it...not letting you go, baby...don't ask me to...*

She wrapped the arm not trapped between them around his neck and held him tightly as her vagina spasmed around his cock. He drove deep one last time and held there, his length jerking violently as he started to come, jetting her full of his hot, creamy seed, his body shaking violently. Under the pressure of his mouth, Jordan sobbed and held him tightly as she felt her body fly over into places she hadn't thought she could ever go. So it wasn't just make-believe—a climax could really make that happen. Her toes curled, her body slowly relaxing as Angelo rolled his hips in the cradle of her thighs and lightened his kiss, brushing softly against her mouth.

Chapter Four

He could feel the slow, heavy pounding of her heart, the blissful satisfaction that flooded her, the almost dazed confusion. The embarrassment.

Angelo...? she kept thinking.

"Hmm," she hummed with pleasure as he lifted his head to study her, her face glowing, damp, her eyes sultry.

"I love you," he said softly, meeting her eyes. "I'm not expecting anything from you once we leave here, but I am going to pursue you, and I will have you. I just thought I should I give you fair warning."

Her pretty, green eyes widened and her mouth parted. "You hardly know me," she stuttered.

One corner of his mouth curled up in a smile. Angelo sighed and shook his head. "I know you. I've always known you Jordan, even before I met you. I knew the minute I saw you climb out of Lee's car that you were with the wrong brother. But he's my brother...what I was supposed to do? Kidnap you? Steal you behind his back? Granted, Lee has no problem operating that way," he mused, remembering. Then he shook his head, threw off old memories. "I think I always knew something would happen, so I could wait. Or maybe I'm just being sentimental. But you weren't right for Lee. And he doesn't deserve you."

He watched as her eyes widened, then fluttered closed while he surged back inside her. "Did he ever, even once, make you feel like this?" he murmured, lowering his head and catching one tightly pearled nipple in his mouth. Her taste, salty now from their loving, but sweet and so *her*, so very…Jordan, intoxicated him. The tight clasp of her sex, wet from her cream, his come…he shuddered with pleasure as he pushed back inside, rising to his knees and gripping her slim hips while pulling her upright and guiding her legs around his waist. "Did he?"

"No," she moaned, rolling her hips against his, catching her lower lip between her teeth and whimpering with sheer pleasure as he used his hold on her hips to pull her completely down, imbedding his thick, burning length inside her. He reached behind her, lubricating his fingers and drawing the moisture up and back, watching her eyes as he started to probe the tiny pucker of her ass.

"You've wanted this…haven't you?" he whispered, his voice a dark rough purr. "And you asked him, but he wouldn't give it. I will."

Jordan moaned as she felt the tip of his finger breech her there, the burning pressure… "Push down," he urged her. She sobbed and caught her breath only to scream seconds later as he slid his finger home inside her ass, the tearing pain of it startling her. "Shhh," he crooned, reaching between her thighs, working her clit with his thumb until her eyes started to glaze. "I know it hurts. Trust me, though, do you trust me?"

"Yes," she moaned and started to rock her hips as he began to withdraw the caress of his thumb on her clit. He'd start again if she moved, but only if she moved. And when she moved, she started to ride his cock and the thick finger he had buried inside her ass…and before she even had time to think, that tearing, burning pressure turned into hot, burning pleasure with every lift and stroke of her hips.

"You like that, huh?" Angelo murmured as she braced her hands on his wide shoulders and started to drive herself down with short, fast strokes. She wailed in frustration when he abruptly pulled her off and left her lying on her back, glaring at him with blank, uncomprehending, frustrated eyes.

He briefly left the room, returning a few seconds later, and her eyes widened when she saw what he held. A bottle she recognized from shopping at adult toy websites—her favorite kind of lubricant, a self-warming kind. A silver bullet, oh, she liked that. And something else she recognized. Hot little licks of excitement tore through her, but they were tinged with fear.

Because he had a seven-inch butt plug in his hand.

"Roll over," he told her, a small smile curving his mouth.

Her mouth was dry.

"Huh?"

"Roll over," he repeated. When she just stared, half fascinated by the butt plug, he said softly, "You want me to give you something Lee would never dream of? I will. I want to. But I won't do it without preparing you first. Now roll over, Jordan."

Angelo smiled gently as her frantic emotions flooded his senses. Half terrified, unbelievably aroused. "Shh," he whispered, stroking his hands down her hips. He bent low over her body and crooned, "I'm gonna make every dream you ever had come true."

She laughed shakily and asked, "Promise?" as she rolled onto her hands and knees. She jumped when she felt his hands stroking her ass. He laughed. "Easy, baby. Take it easy." Her lids fluttered as he pressed the bullet up between her folds. The madly vibrating little device against her swollen, engorged clit pulled a low moan from her lips.

The lubricant was cool at first—very cool—but it heated almost as soon as it touched her flesh. As he started to work one finger inside the tight pucker of her ass, it was hot, tantalizingly so, and she squirmed against him, biting her lip. He slid one brawny arm around her waist, lifting her upright as he moved so that she was between his knees. He took the bullet and held it in place with his palm as he started to pump two fingers in and out of her wet sex while he screwed one in and out of the snug glove of her ass.

"It's tight," he crooned against her ear. "Soft, snug…hot. How long will you let me keep you prisoner, Jordan? Long enough to get you ready for this? Long enough that I can push my cock inside this sweet little tail?" He pushed a second finger inside just as he slid the fingers of his other hand deep and hard into her vagina—ripping a scream from her body, holding her as she arched in climax and screamed wildly.

While she was still riding the wave of it, he pushed her onto her hands and knees, lubricated her anus more, then the butt plug, and started to push it in. "Push down. Now, Jordan," he said harshly when she stiffened and tried to squirm away, even though she was still whimpering and weak from climax. He gripped her hip and held her tightly. "Push down." He watched as the tiny pink hole stretched around the blunt head, and he groaned in agony, his cock jerking in jealous protest. He pushed slowly and steadily, even when she started to whimper and plead.

"Shhh," he whispered. He released her hip and fished the bullet out of the mess of sheets and shoved it into her hand, then guided it to her mound. It fell away and she tried to squirm out of his reach, but he slapped her butt lightly with the flat of his hand. "Don't," he warned. He paused, the butt plug only two inches inside her, just where it was starting to flare, where it was probably burning the most, and pushed the bullet against her clit, holding her hand in place. "Use it." He held his hand over hers until she was actually riding the damn thing, then he went back to inserting the toy inside her snug anus, sliding three more inches into her.

She wailed and squirmed, even as she rocked her hips, helping to take it inside. He gripped the curve of one cheek and pulled, spreading her wide...pushing the toy the final two inches inside and listening as her startled scream bounced off the walls.

Before she could make up her mind whether she hated it or loved it, he gripped her hips and started to burrow his aching cock inside the narrowed passage of her sex, gritting his teeth at the increased resistance.

She sobbed, burying her face against the bed. The burning, pinching pain was entirely too much — and it only grew as Angelo slowly forced his thick length inside her, his big, hard hands gripping her hips and holding her shaking body still. The head of his cock lodged against the mouth of her womb and Jordan moaned roughly as he pulled out and surged back inside, trying to pull away from the increasing fullness as he lodged his thumb against the plug in her ass and started to rhythmically push against it. Once more, she let the bullet fall from her nerveless fingers, her body convulsing from the alternating hot/cold chills that ran through her.

"Stop fighting it, baby," he crooned. "Stop fighting...hmmm. Wet, sweet, silky little pussy. I love it. You have any idea how long I've waited to feel you around me? How long I've waited to bury my cock inside you?"

Jordan whimpered as he released one hip to reach around her, his fingers settling on her hardened clit and stroking. "Relax," he whispered against her ear, easing their bodies down to the bed, slowing his driving thrusts to slow, gentle strokes as he tweaked her clit, massaging it with slow circles until she started to rock her hips against his hand. Seeking out the caress and riding his cock harder at the same time, feeling the thick, rounded head of it stroking her deep inside, everything seemed more deeply sensitized from the toy that was nestled in her ass.

Angelo felt the exact moment it changed from near pain to excruciating pleasure as her body went from tense to wildfire. She started to work herself up and down against his hand, on his cock. Shifting and squirming, she faced away, straddling him as he lay on his back, treating him to a view of her slim little ass and the plug he had pushed inside her.

"Killing me," he muttered, shaking his head, gripping her hips and pushing his cock up inside her.

She screamed and her head fell back.

Reaching around her, he caught her breast, tweaking one stiff, hard nipple as he sat up, and shimmied up in the bed. Planting his back against the headboard and cupping a breast in each hand, he pinched her nipples lightly, then more firmly, until he felt the shudder rack her body. She started to ride him, the tight, wet clasp of her sheath on his cock driving him to near insanity.

The phantom touch of her fingers on his sac, the light vibrations…she had found the bullet again and had placed it against her clit and now she was pumping her hips harder and harder. Hot, breathy little moans were falling from her mouth, her short, spiked hair damp with sweat, her heart pounding against his palm as he pulled her back against his chest and sank his teeth into the curve where neck and shoulder joined.

She moaned and shuddered as the tiny little muscles in her vagina started to milk him, slowly at first, and then faster and harder, until Angelo's eyes nearly crossed with the pleasure of it and he was groaning out her name as he pumped her full of his come, wrapping his big arms around her slim waist, burying his face against her neck.

Jordan whimpered in weak protest as he pulled the toy from her ass. It hurt—she flinched and bit her lip, hiding her blush against the pillow as he padded naked into the bathroom. She pretended to be asleep when he came back after turning off the water and stood there staring down at her with a cocked eyebrow. But when he picked her up and rubbed his stubbled face against her neck, she squealed and batted at him and stopped pretending, glaring at him.

"Shower," he said, shrugging his wide shoulders, smiling affably.

"Sleep," she replied drolly.

"Shower," he said in the same tone, setting her down and cupping her sex, which was wet with her cream and his semen. "So after sleep I can eat."

She was blushing as she responded, "Okay. Shower."

She had never showered with a man. Not that she hadn't wanted to. But Lee...well, romance hadn't been his strong suit. And Jordan had come to believe she just didn't inspire that in a guy. But in less than three minutes, under the pulsating dual shower heads, Angelo did more than make up for months of what she was coming to realize had been neglect on Lee's part—not a lack in her. She whimpered in pleasure as Angelo massaged her scalp, working her favorite shampoo into her hair. Angelo nudged her under the showerhead and rinsed her hair then worked conditioner through and repeated the rinsing process once more before reaching for her soap.

Her favorite, of course.

How had he known?

He hadn't been expecting her...which meant while she was sleeping he had gone out and gotten it.

Lee wouldn't have made that special trip.

Lee wouldn't have done a lot of things.

She happened to glance up and saw a grim light in Angelo's eyes. "Darlin', do me a favor. I realize the thoughts you're thinking are favorable to me, and not my brother, but stop thinking of him. You think of him, and I hear those thoughts, clear as day. And I don't like it. If I hear his name one more time..."

A feral snarl darkened his face and his mouth crushed down on hers, stealing her breath as he pinned her against the wall of the shower stall, lifting her up and spreading her thighs, piercing her and driving his cock home in one quick, hard thrust. Then he met her eyes, his own dark and hungry and shadowed. "You're mine, you should have always been mine," he rasped, settling his hips into a heavy, driving rhythm as he gripped her thighs and held them wide open. "And you thinking of Lee, in any way, reminds me that he had you, that he fucked you. And it infuriates me."

His tongue drove past the barrier of her lips, filled her mouth, thrusting and filling her as his cock pounded into her weeping cleft. Jordan's hands clutched at his shoulders and she held on for dear life, shivering as he shifted his grip on her and scraped his thumb over her clit. As he pulled his mouth from hers, the deep sucking kiss left her panting and gasping for air.

The thick, rounded head of his cock rubbed against the bundled bed of nerves buried by the mouth of her womb, while he rubbed his wet chest against hers, causing her nipples to tighten and throb and her breath to catch in her throat. Her head fell limply back against the wall of the shower stall and she sobbed out his name as he stared down at her with dark, hungry eyes.

"He won't ever touch you again," Angelo hissed, driving deep. Thrust.

"Ever fuck you." Thrust.

"You're mine." Thrust.

Jordan wailed as he pinched her clit roughly, the orgasm seemingly ripped from her body.

"Say it." Thrust.

"Say it." Thrust and retreat.

She shivered and screamed as she arched against him, pushing her hips up and out, working herself against his cock as best she could with him gripping her with his arm beneath her ass.

"Mine, damn it," he rasped, settling his teeth in the flesh of her neck and marking her. "Say it."

Thrust and retreat…slower.

"Yours," she whimpered, tightening the muscles of her pussy around him and trying to hold his cock inside her this time.

His control shattered and he pounded into her, hard and fast, while her screams echoed off the walls and filled the bathroom. A second orgasm tore through her, and her convulsing sheath locked down on his cock. He had to work his turgid length inside her against the tightening channel as she came.

Angelo pushed in to the hilt and held there, legs spread wide, braced, back arched as his cock jerked and pumped. As his semen spurted into her body, the wild jealousy and fury slowly seeped out of him and washed down the drain.

He let himself read her hesitantly, unaware of what he was going to feel from her. The mind-numbing pleasure was somewhat reassuring, but…fuck.

Still.

"I'm sorry," he said softly, stroking his hand down her wet arm, reaching for the faucet and turning off the water before fumbling just outside for a towel and flicking it over her still shuddering body.

"…huh?"

"I didn't…shouldn't have done that," he said slowly, rubbing her with the towel until her soft, slim body was dry and glowing. His lean, tanned cheeks flushed a dull red and he had to force himself to meet her eyes. "I didn't have any right—" he paused to blow out a long shallow breath, reaching behind his neck and rubbing the taut muscles. "Do you have any idea how much I've hated seeing you with him?" he asked quietly.

Slowly, Jordan said, "A better idea now than I did ten minutes ago."

He narrowed his eyes on her face, glimpsing the tiny spark that was there, then gone in her pretty, green eyes. Her elfin face was glowing, her mouth curved up and she looked rather…pleased. "He never once touched me like that," she said, letting him see just how much she had yearned for it. "Not once. And I needed it."

She closed the small distance between them and wrapped her arms around his neck. Pressing her lips to his mouth, Jordan whispered, "Don't, Angelo. Don't. I've never felt needed, until just now. Don't regret it."

"How long have you had these…new gifts?" she asked later that night. "What all can you do?"

He stroked one hand down her back and sighed. "Ten years," he admitted, shaking his head. "Ten fucking years. Lee has his head so stuck in his own business it never dawned on him to care. And as to what…it's not just empathy anymore. I can speak into your mind as well as his. I think it has to be somebody I feel a bond with — but I can do it more and more. And I don't have to be touching people to pick up on their emotions. I just have to be within range. Within sight, or the same room."

"That's why you've gotten so many new jobs," she murmured. "He says it's because people are willing to try anything when they are desperate, and that you just get lucky. But it's the new gifts."

"And I'm a good investigator. Sometimes I don't even have to use the gift," he said, scowling at the thought of

Lee. "He's supposed to be learning the ropes and all he does is PR and budgets and bookkeeping. Fine by me — that way I don't have to. But how he can talk about my job when he's never bothered to learn it?"

"Tell me about the kids," she whispered, stroking one hand absently over his chest.

"No" he whispered, shaking his head.

She peered up at him in the dim light and asked, "Why not? I'm not looking for a story or anything. I just want to know." He never talked to the media or anyone outside the cops or the kid's families about those he helped bring home. But she wanted to know.

"Because it hurts," he said gruffly. "And I don't want to think of painful things when I have everything I've ever wanted right here." He rolled her over and pinned her under him, kissing her, gently at first, and then with growing hunger. "Ask me again...some other time. But not now, not here."

Early the next morning, Jordan looked toward Angelo hesitantly.

He was cheerful, whistling, and carrying on as though it was just an average day.

And her whole world felt like it was changing. The careful, cautious way she had always done things didn't feel like the right way to continue —

"Because it's not," he said almost absently, as he tossed bacon into a skillet.

She stared at him over her coffee cup, the thick mug halfway to her lips. He paused and said, "Oops." He had the grace to flush and shrug half-heartedly. "You're ah, kinda broadcast thinking there."

Lowering the cup, she asked, "I've always been careful. If that's not right, then what is? And why isn't it right?"

He lowered the fork he had been using to jab at the raw bacon and said softly, "Jordan, you've always been careful because people expected you to be. Not because you wanted to be. Deep down inside you've always wanted to leap before looking, haven't you?" He turned off the stove before shifting around and leaning back against the counter to face her, folding his arms across his sculpted, naked chest. "You wanted to paint rainbows and faeries, and were told to do mathematical equations. You wanted to write books, but your parents said it was more profitable to sell them."

"And Lee?" she asked. "What about Lee?"

Angelo's mouth lifted in a half smile. "Lee was safe, too. He didn't make you think too hard, didn't make you feel too much. I will, Jordan," he promised. "I'll take everything and I'll give everything. I'll push you to your limits and I'll make you feel everything you're capable of feeling. I don't believe in safe zones, Jordan."

Chapter Five

Jordan knew she had never felt as wicked as she did right now, straddling his big, black and chrome Harley, while Angelo stood watching her naked body. She was wearing the black boots he had brought out, and she suspected he had a few more things in store, but right now, she was quivering inside just from the vibrations of the bike.

And his dark brown eyes on her.

"That bike would almost make your vibrator obsolete, wouldn't it?" he purred, pacing a slow circle around her, watching as she squirmed, and her eyes glazed as she leaned forward and shifted, so that her clit was in contact with the leather of the seat—*oh, damn*…her teeth sank into her lip and she jumped when she felt one big warm hand close over her rump.

And then, something else probing. Something rounded, cool, cock-shaped. "Let's add something else to the mix," he teased as he started to shallowly thrust a dildo into her wet cleft. "It drove me crazy, knowing what you were thinking, feeling you plastered against me while driving you home. All I wanted to do was pull over and strip you naked and bend you over. Like you are now."

She was bent over the bike, face towards the rear wheel, ass up, whimpering, squirming, biting her lip as he pushed the slender dildo deeper inside. "And that's how we're gonna end up, baby," he teased as she sobbed out his name. "We've got a few more fantasies of yours left to fill and isn't that one of them?"

"Angelo," she whimpered against the leather, the cool night air caressing her heated skin, body aching, tight. Hungry.

The slim toy left her cleft, trailed upward, and she jumped as it started to probe the tight pucker of her ass. Her breath caught in her throat and she pushed down without him telling her to as he started to press it against her. It slid inside easier than the thicker plug had, and she sighed a shivery little sigh at the exquisite sensation that slid through her as he started to work it in and out.

Moments later, she felt him straddle the seat behind her and she squirmed forward just a little, resting her body on the bike. She jerked in surprise though when she felt him catch her hands, cuffing them at the small of her back.

"You wanted to be a prisoner," Angelo teased, sliding the key into his pocket, staring down at her in the pale silvery glow of moonlight. Through the spiky fall of her bangs, he could see her wide eyes, and the hesitant, excited gleam there. *Fuck, Lee, why in the hell couldn't you play a little?* he wondered. And then, *Shit, damn good thing you didn't.* He shallowly thrust the slender wand-like dildo in and out of her snug little anus a few times with one hand as he unfastened his jeans. "Hope no cops decide to check on the cabin. They do every once in a while. To make sure no kids came by to party. Of course, they see you, they might want to party."

The hot, little flash of excitement he felt from her had him grinning. "Naughty, Jordan. You got a thing for group fucks?"

"No," she replied smartly, pushing her hips back against him. "But I've had dreams about threesomes." Then she ruined her sassy comeback by whimpering, "Angelo, please..."

He pushed the thick head of his cock into the sheath of her vagina, shuddering at the sensation of her tight, creamy sex closing around him. As he pushed deeper inside, he released his hold on the wand in her ass, letting his lower belly push it back inside her. Stroking his hands up her arms and down around to cup her breasts, he murmured, "Not a threesome, maybe, but how does that feel?" he whispered.

Her answer was a long, ragged moan as he pulled out, the wand retreating with him, then he drove back inside in long powerful thrusts that stole her breath. "Not sure how I'd feel about sharing you, even for a night," he muttered, shifting his grip to her hips, settling into a hard-driving rhythm, bracing his heels into the earth. His sac was already drawn tight against him, and he swore, fighting off the need to come. "Of course, maybe once, with Lee, to let him know what a fool he was—no, he ain't ever touching you again." He drove harder into her.

Jordan gasped, her hands clenching into fists within the restraining cuffs. "Don't...want him," she whispered. Hot little flames licked at her belly as the climax built inside. She could feel him driving deep inside her wet cleft, could feel the slender wand slicing through the tender tissues of her ass, both exquisite sensations, and all the while, beneath her, the bike rumbled and vibrated. Every down stroke pushed her against the seat, exposing her clit to the powerful vibrations, bringing a sob to her lips.

She felt him reaching beneath her, opening the lips of her sex, exposing her clit even more to the vibrations of the bike. She screamed as he pushed her down, filling her with hard, short driving thrusts of his cock, and sending the wand deeper and harder into her tender ass. Exploding with a vicious, agonizing scream, her nails digging into her skin, she pushed her hips back and up against him, taking him as deep and hard as she could.

He filled her with hot, heavy, wet bursts of semen, each jerk of his cock making her quiver as she milked him dry.

"Mmmm," he hummed into her hair as he bent over her, stroking his hands down her naked hips. He was still fully clothed, jeans on, shirt on, but unbuttoned. He nuzzled her neck and whispered into her ear, "I never thought I'd enjoy having a prisoner."

She giggled. "Hopefully, I'm the only one you plan on having. I'm kinda enjoying this. I'd like this to be a full-time occupation," she said and then she yawned. "You're exhausting me."

He laughed. "Either that or boring you," he said, shaking his head. He straightened and caressed her naked back before fishing the key out of his pocket.

He was uncuffing her as she said softly, "No. Not that. This is the furthest from bored I've ever been in my life." Once her hands were free, she shifted and squirmed until she could cuddle up against him. Curling one hand into the loose material of his shirt, she nuzzled her cheek against his chest, listening to his pounding heart. "I didn't think I could feel like this."

Stroking her naked back, he rested his cheek on hers. "Lee's an idiot."

"Wasn't him. It was me, for thinking he was right for me," she said. She was too embarrassed to say it out loud, or to even hope that maybe he felt that he was as right for her as she thought him to be, but she didn't have to say a damn thing. He could hear, and feel, every damn thought flowing through her mind and body, as close as they were.

"Damn it, Jordan," he groaned, threading his fingers through her short spiky cap of hair, molding his hands to her skull and holding her head still as he kissed her, pushing his tongue deep inside her mouth. *Always you*, he whispered inside her mind.

I knew it the first time I saw you. I love you.

There was nothing like having a lover who could feel and sense your every thought and desire. *Nothing.*

Jordan whimpered as he positioned her on her hands and knees. The lubricant was warmed by his hands as he started to rub it on her anus, then push his fingers inside her. She sobbed and her body tensed uncontrollably as one thick finger entered her.

The pain of it was sweet, hot and burning as he thrust in and out. She cried out as he pressed the bullet against her clit, making her hips buck madly. She started to rock against it, riding his fingers as he pushed a second one in. *Oh, hell,* she thought mindlessly her hips rocking faster and faster —

Then he stopped.

She wailed in frustration and pushed back, only to feel the thick, blunt head of his cock probing her rosette. "Hush," Angelo whispered as she whimpered in fear. He stroked one hand down her back, gripped the smooth curve of one cheek and pulled her open, stretching her, easing the way as he started to push inside. "Push down for me, Jordan."

She cried out as he pushed deep inside her, past the tight ring of muscle. One arm reached around her waist, pulling her back against him snugly while he used his other hand to reach between her thighs and spread the lips of her sex open, pushing back the hood of flesh and stroking her clit with firm rapid strokes until she stopped focusing on the pain so much, and started to rock against his hand.

Each tiny movement of her hips took his cock deep inside the satin-slicked entrance of her ass in tiny little increments that had Angelo sweating and swearing under his breath as he focused on her. He no longer felt the pain and nerves flowing from her so he started to push his aching cock up into her, groaning raggedly when she mewled and pushed back hungrily, only to lift herself off, following the movement of his fingers on her clit.

He pushed her back onto her hands and knees and gripped her hips, staring down at the sight of his cock sliding home inside her ass. The tender, pink flesh stretched tight around him as he pulled out and pushed back in, his hands clenching her hips tightly. She fell forward onto her chest and Angelo swore as he picked up on her movements, sensed that she was stroking her clit, then sliding her fingers in and out of her cream-soaked vagina while she panted and sobbed out his name.

"You're tighter, hotter, sweeter than anything I've ever felt in my life," he rasped as he pulled out and drove back into her, slamming home and shuddering as she tightened around him and gasped. He could feel what it did to her, the sweet, hot licks of pleasure-pain that licked through her each time he thrust into her. It was mind numbing, feeling both his pleasure, and hers. His eyes slitted and his sac drew tight against him as he fought the urge to pound himself into her and come, ending this first encounter.

"Angelo," she wailed as he settled into a hard, steady rhythm, gritting his teeth, his head falling back, eyes closed.

I think I love you...

He went mad.

She didn't say it out loud.

But then, she didn't have to.

Shoving her hips low, he pounded his thick cock inside her, bending low over her body, setting his teeth into her shoulder and growling manically as she reached back and grabbed a fistful of his hair. The powerful muscles in his hips, back and legs propelled him as he jackhammered into her, feeling her ass start to clench and convulse around him.

Pulling his mouth from her shoulder, he growled against her ear, "Come, Jordan. Scream my name, and come for me."

She was already sobbing out his name, and the muscles inside her virgin ass were clenching down with climax as he pushed his way back inside and started to come, his cock jerking viciously as he pumped his semen inside her. She vised down and started to climax, screaming as he worked a hand underneath her, then pumped two thick fingers in and out of her creamy swollen sex.

He pushed his cock in to the hilt, and held firm, groaning as the spasms ripping through her milked him dry. Burying his face against her neck, he groaned and wrapped one arm around her, holding her tightly. She worked her arms around his, so that she cuddled his arm to her chest while she sobbed out his name, then sighed it as he rolled them onto their sides.

Chapter Six

When they both opened their eyes, they realized they had an audience of one.

Lee stood in the door staring at them, his eyes flashing with fury.

And Jordan giggled.

"Isn't this poetic justice," she drawled, snuggling back against Angelo.

Angelo pushed up onto his elbow and snagged a sheet from the tangle at the foot of the bed, flipping it over Jordan before he gently eased out of her, soothing her with a kiss on her nape as she flinched. "If you've a need to talk to us, Lee, you can wait in the other room while we take a shower," Angelo offered, still reclining on the bed.

"Was this to get back at me, Jordan?" Lee asked coolly.

"What? This? No. I'm not a slut, who will go sleeping with a man for any old reason. I slept with Angelo because I wanted him," she said, smiling sleepily up at the man in question, not even feeling a flare of anger towards her ex-fiancé. "And he wants me, more than you ever did. All you ever wanted me for was my money, wasn't it, Lee? And, no, before you ask, Angelo hasn't said anything. I didn't ask, he didn't tell. I put two and two together. I'm a smart girl. You like money, you wanted more, and I have it."

He didn't even bother to deny it. "We're a good match, Jordan. Neither of us are the type to get overly emotional about—"

She cocked a brow at him. "I don't know. I was emotional a few minutes ago." Her heart was still racing from it. "And I intend to get in that state as often as I can."

Lee sneered. "I thought you were more refined than that. If it's a good butt-fuck you want, I can give it to you. I thought you were asking for something you couldn't handle, but I'm willing to play whatever games you want to try," he drawled.

"Watch it," Angelo said softly, sitting up and pinning Lee with a warning stare. "You've been sitting at a desk, playing businessman for a long time, Lee. You've gotten soft. And I'm trying to remember you're my blood, my twin. I'm trying to remember that. But if you aren't careful, I'll forget."

Lee opened his mouth, and then stomped away, swearing under his breath.

Jordan was still smiling.

Angelo stared at her.

Shrugging, she said, "That's more emotion than I've ever seen from him. But I think it's over the money. Not me. It's sad that he can't care about a person that way."

* * * * *

Twenty minutes later, showered, wearing one of Angelo's shirts, she met with Lee in the living room, meeting his eyes squarely, with Angelo standing at her back. She lifted her chin and reached up, lacing the fingers of one hand with the fingers that Angelo stroked over her shoulder.

"Let's head this off first—I'm not going back with you. I'm not marrying you. You've had three days to get your things out of *my* house. As to what constitutes your things, they are the things you purchased with your money, or our money. I won't fight over any of that. But if one thing that was there before you came is gone, I will hurt you badly. All of my stuff is listed on my insurance policy, so don't bother trying to be petty that way," she warned.

"Oh, he won't, will you, brother?" Angelo asked.

"I'm not planning on leaving here without you, Jordan," Lee said lazily, staring at her with hooded eyes.

"You don't have a choice," she said shrugging. "I don't want to be with you."

"So you'd give up a good marriage for a couple of fucks with him?" Lee sneered. "Angelo is little more than a vagrant."

"Angelo is the man I should have been with all along," she replied. "He's a better man than you by far. I bet I'd never walk in on him fucking another woman. And I'm curious—if your so-called psychic gifts are so fucking powerful, so much better than Angelo's, how come you didn't know I was there at the house before I caught you?"

Angelo smiled slowly. "Lee is good at putting people on. He has a built-in compass, he can locate people through things that he's touched. And he can read your thoughts if he's touching you. He picks up random thoughts from strangers on a regular basis, but there's no consistency to it. And he and I can speak mind to mind, but he's not the swami he'd like you to think," Angelo drawled. "That's why he's the businessman and I'm the locator and investigator. If I'd known what a shabby partner I was taking on…I thought he would at least try normal means of investigating."

Lee flushed angrily, shoving up off the chair. "Jordan, this is bullshit. Come on, let's go home and talk this out," he insisted.

"No. I want Angelo. I'm falling in love with him. And he loves me. He always has," she said, her eyes wide with the wonder of that. "He really, truly loves *me*. And you never did. Why would I give that up?"

They barely heard the sound of the door slamming as Jordan turned to face Angelo, lifting her face for a kiss, holding him tight to her.

Why would I give you up? she thought, knowing he would hear her.

He held her tightly against him as he turned and pressed her to the wall. Pulling his mouth away, and kissing his way to her ear, he murmured, "You're still my prisoner, baby. What makes you think you've got a choice?"

She laughed as she fisted her hands in his hair. "Make sure my parole hearing isn't for a good century, at least," she suggested. "I'll be on real bad behavior anyway."

"Do you promise?"

She giggled and boosted herself up, wrapping her legs around him. "Absolutely," she purred, rubbing against him. "I'll be as bad as I know how to be. But, you'll probably have to teach me."

MYTHE: SATYR

Introduction

I was browsing the web a few months ago, searching for information on Greek mythology. I had this idea for a new work involving elves, angels, and vampires. I saw a lot of wonderful pictures, one in particular of this unbelievably beautiful Satyr. I started seeing a picture of this Satyr in my mind, so sad, so lost, seeking his own mate.

Daklin's story was actually the one I meant to write first, but Arys planted himself so firmly in my head, I simply couldn't get him out.

His story is the introduction to the world I have created. The fantastical world of Mythe. It is not a complete story in itself, but it wasn't meant to be.

I hope you enjoy it. I hope it intrigues you enough to be as hungry to read more of the world of Mythe as I am to write it. Now, please join me as we enter MYTHE...

Chapter One
In a World Called Mythe

Arys used to love to look through the Gates to the other world. He had since he was but a young thing, all big eyes and two nubby horns on his skull, while his mother teased and chided him for his endless curiosity.

But he was a satyr, wasn't he? Satyrs were supposed to be curious. And mischievous, and devious, and according to some, even downright evil...

But Arys was a satyr who had more or less forgotten how to laugh, and he no longer cared about the other world, the Gates, or the fact that he had been charged with watching this one in his wood.

A year ago today, his wife had died.

Lorne had fallen sick to a fever while carrying their first child and the Healers in the Cyruon hadn't cared enough to save a female satyr who was having trouble with her babe.

None of the Healers who had been around had believed Arys when he had told them he was a Gatekeeper. The Healer who had heard of his plight and knew him had arrived too late, and Lorne had already died, along with their unborn child. Arys had retreated to his wood and hadn't left since.

He would not have a choice now. The Council was calling a Summit, and as one of the Gatekeepers, Arys had no choice but to go. He absently rubbed the scar on his palm before turning to study the wood behind him. The scar marked him as a Gatekeeper, and his blood had flowed from the wound that had formed the scar, binding him. Not to the wood — his birth had done that — but to the Gate that was inside the wood.

He ran a hand through his sable hair, fingering one of the two horns that curved upward from his scalp. He moved into his *iskita* and started to prepare for his journey, his heart feeling heavy. Once he would have looked forward to such a journey, to the adventure, to seeing people he knew were friends. The elvin lord, Daklin, Gatekeeper in the elvish realms, was a wry, droll character, nearly as curious about the mortal realms as Arys had once been.

Ronal de Ahmshe, the vampire lord, Gatekeeper in his territory far, far north was almost frightening, but very intriguing. And the women he brought with him...once, before Arys had wed Lorne, those women had been the light of the world.

And Cray, the fallen one. Some whispered that he truly was an angel fallen from heaven. Some said he was a messenger. Some said he was one of the Lord's henchmen. Some said he was one of the evil ones. But Cray was a friend to Arys, and had been one of the few who had offered true sympathy and comfort after Lorne had died.

There were others, but those three, the other three Pillar Gatekeepers, were his truest friends. The Pillar Gates were the largest ones, the ones that had the most refugees from the mortal realm falling through them. And the ones with the most criminals from Arys' realm trying to escape into the mortal realm where they could use their various magicks to hide and wreak havoc on the more helpless mortals there.

Arys scoffed at the thought. *Helpless my fucking hooves,* he thought, glancing at the two cloven appendages his legs ended in. They might not have the magick in the mortal realms that his world had, but they were not helpless. The weapons alone could destroy their own planet. As he recalled some of the things he had learned during his time as a Gatekeeper, some four decades now, the poor broken children who had tumbled through his Gate, the battered women, the hopeless men, all thinking life had simply run out.

Maybe they are right, Arys thought bleakly, taking a wrap and clothing himself. He sometimes wore it in his wood, not often. But sometimes. Since he was taking to the public roads though, the humans and the other inhabitants of his world seemed to have a problem seeing an unclothed satyr in their midst. Like he was likely to fall on their women and ravish them.

Arys was in no mood to ravish any woman.

He simply wanted his wife and child back.

His swarthy face etched with grief, he didn't hear the soft whicker behind him until the unicorn had already entered his *iskita* and brushed his velvety nose across Arys' arm, reaching out with a silent mental touch. *What ails my brother?*

Arys looked at Faryn and smiled sadly. "The same thing that has ailed me for the past twelve moons, my friend," he said hoarsely, closing his eyes and trying vainly to shove his grief aside. "I did not know you were coming so close to the Gate, Faryn."

Something feels amiss, the stallion said, tossing his head in an equine shrug.

"A refugee?"

No, Faryn mused, cocking his head. The horn—silver, swirled with gold—glinted in the dim light. *But not one of the black ones trying to escape us either. Some one from THERE is trying to open it.*

THERE could only be one place. The mortal realms. Arys shook his head. "The mortals do not know how to open the Gates. The Gates open as they see fit."

They have been opened before, Faryn said, shrugging again. *But I felt a disturbance and I came to see.* His bluer-than-blue eyes turned to study Arys and he looked as sorrowful as an eternal creature could. *I grieve to know that you still hurt, young satyr. Lorne would hate to know that you are still grieving. She is no longer suffering, know that. She is in a place where she is ever young and happy and well.*

Arys turned away and blocked his thoughts automatically. *And she is in a place where I am not,* he added. *A place where I cannot touch her, smell her, mount her and sink my cock inside her sweet sheath. A place where she is beyond my reach. I shall never know my child, or know another moment's happiness.*

The stallion made a low thrumming sound in his deep chest, hanging his head over Arys' chest, and the satyr realized he had not kept his thoughts deep enough. In the equine embrace, he grieved as the unicorn softly whispered into his mind. *Now that, my young satyr, is simply not true. You shall know happiness. And it shall be soon.*

Chapter Two
In the Mortal Realm

Her sweaty red curls fell into her face as Pepper lowered her aching arms. It had almost worked. *Almost.* There was something out there, something she could almost feel, almost see, almost touch. It lingered, like a forgotten name, on the tip of her magick, and she knew, just *knew*, if she tried a little harder, she'd have it.

With a sigh, she plopped down on her butt and reached for her robe.

Practicing magick in the nude was not helping.

The silver cross between her breasts was cold and damp. Glancing down, she said, "There's nothing wrong with being naked. But I feel silly, like some wanna-be Wiccan dancing in the forest."

There was nothing wanna-be about Pepper St. John. Her birth certificate said Patrice St. John. But she had been Pepper since she was a baby. She'd had magick for about as long.

And she didn't call herself a Wiccan or a witch.

She had magick.

But she went to church, and she read the Bible. She believed in heaven and hell, and a whole slew of other things that had caused her to be laughed at the few times she had gone to meetings of others like her. Some of them had fancied themselves to be magick. And they had always considered themselves to be so very accepting. But they had scoffed at her beliefs. When she had honestly, but politely, told them she didn't believe in the Goddess, they had stared at her.

"Then where does your magick come from?" one had asked her. Because in order to walk into the meeting, she had first had to prove she had the magick.

She had shrugged and said, "God."

They had snickered. Some had rolled their eyes.

Pepper had left a few minutes later.

That had been a while ago, maybe two years now? Since then she had been practicing on her own, using the magick to do what good she could, where she could. She went to church, religiously even, she thought to herself with a grin as she cleaned up the candles. They were more for the calming influence than for any other reason. Besides, she loved the look and smell of them.

Other than the fact that she could levitate and make things dance in mid-air, or make the money from a deadbeat dad's wallet end up in his ex-wife's purse, Pepper liked to think she was your average run-of-the-mill woman. So what if she was able to occasionally locate a missing child—not psychically, of course, magickally— and have that child go back to their parents?

And it had been almost an accident when she had set fire to the house a few doors down from a co-workers home, where the man had set up a meth lab. Not a big fire or anything. But it had gotten the firemen and the cops into the house.

And now one more drug dealer was off the streets.

Well, actually this one made ten.

She was a librarian, she loved kids, worked out, ate junk food—

Except for the past month.

She had woken from a dream, a dream about a man so handsome, so exotic. So sad. Looking at him gave her thoughts that should have sent her to confession. Of course, she wasn't Catholic. Long, thick black hair, a dark swarthy face with a wide, sculpted mouth and black eyes. Those eyes had her enthralled — larger than a man's should be, tilted up, lashed with ridiculously long lashes.

And so sad...

He had been real.

And something inside her said he needed her.

So she did what any other woman who had her talents would do. She used the magick. But the only thing she could discover was some odd...tension in the air. Like the feeling in the air right before lightning strikes, thick, hot, heavy. There was something behind it, an answer.

Pepper knew it.

Stomping out of the den, she headed for the shower. There were answers, answers to the riddle about that man. That extraordinary man. She just had to find them.

* * * * *

Arys awoke early the next morning, irritable, unrested. A woman had invaded his dreams. A mortal woman. Thick, dark-red curls around a young, heart-shaped face, freckles sprinkled across an upturned nose, a sweet rounded mouth...the opposite of Lorne in every way. He rose from his bed, his cloven feet hitting the floor lightly as he sat scowling into space.

Faryn had made him wait.

"The Council is not going to like me not arriving on time. Shall I tell them a Unicorn has requested my presence?" he had mocked scathingly as he stomped back into his *iskita* and tossed his pack back onto the bed, flopping onto his belly while the 'corn poked his white and gray head through the window to wink at him.

A Unicorn's request is more important than a person's, Arys. Please, there is something about.

"Something about, all right," Arys decided as he stared out the open window into the cloud-studded sky. "A meddlesome 'corn is about. What are you up to, Faryn?"

I? Not I, satyr. It is not I that tries to meddle with the Gate, Faryn called to Arys' mind, from out in the yard. *Out of your bed already — you like too many mortal trappings. Why do you not sleep on the sweet earth?*

"You don't sleep on the sweet earth either when you can help it," Arys replied. "You'd prefer to have a silk mattress beneath your hooves if you had your choice." He started to gather his bathing supplies but an odd ripple floated through the air.

"What in the name of Hell?" he whispered as the mark on his hand started to itch.

The Gate. Come, Gatekeeper. Come, Faryn insisted, appearing at the door and presenting his back. *Mount up. I move quicker than even a satyr.*

The cloven-hoofed riding the four-footed, Arys mused as he mounted the 'corn. "What a story this would make," he remarked absently, weaving his hands through the silken mane. It did not feel at all coarse.

No. Because you will not tell. It must not get out that a 'corn let a satyr on his back, instead of only nimble young virgins, Faryn remarked.

Once, Arys would have had much to say about that. Once. Now he just shrugged. "You've no use for a mortal, human virgin anyway. What does it matter if it is I on your back, or a woman?"

For one, her hide would be a shade lighter, I would imagine, Faryn said. The unicorn waited a moment for some mischievous rejoinder, some sign that the joking satyr still lived inside this man, but there was nothing.

If Arys noticed the stallion's silent disappointment, he didn't remark on it as they raced through the wood. Arys' black hair billowed behind him like a banner, his eyes narrowed, watering from the incredible speed. He squeezed his muscled thighs around Faryn's barrel and gripped his mane with strong hands, holding tightly. A 'corn male, full grown and in his prime, could run like the wind.

And Arys didn't care to be thrown.

You ride like you were born to do so, Faryn remarked approvingly.

"Hmmm." The Gate mark on his hand was burning, truly burning now. As he bent low over the 'corn's neck, Arys whispered gruffly, "The Gate is trying to open."

I feel it, Faryn assured him as he breached the barrier that surrounded the Gate. It was unseen by all eyes but the Gatekeeper, the Watchers, and the magick wielders. The Watchers were the sensitives, like Faryn and other unicorns and magicked beasts, and some humans.

If only all those magick wielders were good people —

Arys had a bad feeling that whoever was on the other side of the Gate wasn't a decent sort. Magick rarely came so easily to human hands, and when it did, it was almost always foul hands that held it. Arys kicked one cloven foot over Faryn's back and slid to the ground, striding to the center of the Gate and staring up.

What he saw startled him.

Made his breath catch.

And to his surprise, it made his cock harden.

Through the wavering visage the Gate afforded, he could see a woman, sweet, innocent looking, with tumbled red hair, a heart-shaped face, her eyes closed, her mouth moving silently, arms upthrust. She was naked, gloriously so, her round, firm breasts topped with small pink nipples. A narrow, trim waist, full rounded hips, red curls covering her mound. She was seated and she was alone and there was no evil feel to her.

And as he watched, the Gate opened.

Of its own accord.

She didn't do it.

"What in the name of —"

He felt the heavy nudge at his back as Faryn shoved him forward.

* * * * *

A low, burning-hot feeling ripped through her belly and satisfaction flooded her. Pepper grinned as she felt something give, and open. That heavy, foggy sensation that obscured something magickal was gone and that something magickal lay…

She was falling, falling, falling…

Light swirled and danced around her. Pain flooded her mind and body. A scream was ripped from her throat only to die before it left her mouth. A soundless sob stole her breath, blocked her throat and kept her from gasping for air as she struggled to grab onto something as she continued to fall. The floor was no longer beneath her.

Pepper couldn't smell the vanilla and lavender candles any more, couldn't even hear Enya singing in the background.

She felt herself land against something hard, heard something distant and muffled.

But the pain inside her head won out and she slid into unconsciousness.

* * * * *

Arys stumbled back, and if Faryn hadn't been standing behind him, bracing him with his massive girth, the satyr suspected he would have crashed to the ground. He was strong, incredibly so, but catching a full-grown woman, falling through the mortal realm and into his arms...

He had found people who had fallen through the Gate with bones broken, head injuries, and the like. A trip through the gate was not an easy one. And he hadn't ever been here for any other arrival.

He slid Faryn a narrow look, his thick, silken hair falling into his dark eyes. "What have we here?" he murmured, more to himself than to the unicorn.

A mortal?

A warm, sweet-smelling *female* mortal. Arys' heart kicked up a beat as her scent flooded his head, the soft feel of her skin against his body made him think of things he had not thought of outside of dreams for months. A satyr wasn't designed for a sexless existence. That was laughable.

A rough growl escaped him and his thickly lashed eyes closed. "You knew of this, somehow you knew," he said to Faryn as he started in the direction of his *iskita*. "I do not know *how*, but you knew."

I? Faryn asked innocently, batting his lashes at Arys' back.

"Do not act the innocent, you bloody unicorn," Arys said flatly, trying to ignore the hardening of his cock. Failing miserably. "It suits you as well as it suits me."

You mean as well as this sexless existence suits you? Faryn asked, tossing his head and trotting to catch up with the satyr.

"If you brought me a mortal woman just so I can fuck her, then you owe her an apology," Arys growled. "She can never go back—"

I brought no one here. The unicorn stopped trotting and glared angrily, arrogantly at the satyr. *I haven't that kind of power. Do you truly think that people are brought across the Gate simply for sport? It's never been for that, and well you know it.*

But be a bloody fool and ignore the gift that was given to you.

Faryn turned and leaped nimbly across the brush, disappearing into the wood without another thought or word, his silence letting Arys know just how deeply his thoughtless words had cut.

"Fuck. All I want is to be left alone," he muttered.

Chapter Three

The tearing pain she remembered had faded. Throbbing aches remained. But she could handle those. She wasn't sure how to handle the unfamiliar feel of the bed beneath her.

It felt like nothing she had ever known before.

Like air. But more solid.

Like gel. But softer.

The bed was covered with warmed silk, and more of that warmed silk covered her. A rich, sensual scent—musky, male, and arousing—clung to the bedclothes and filled her head. She drew a slow breath in and felt her nipples harden just from the scent. The fog retreated a bit further from her brain as well, and Pepper was able to remember a little more of what had happened.

The magick had worked.

What it had done, she didn't know. She had opened something. Or maybe she had moved herself somewhere.

That seemed a bit more likely. Okay. So she might as well open her eyes, she decided, and figure out where she was. Then she had to get some clothes, some cash and get herself back home. Cuz *no way, no how* was she trying that bit again in reverse. Her head still felt like it was likely to explode, implode and fall apart all at the same time. Going back the way she'd come was sooo not an option.

A low, musical voice, oddly accented, dangerously sexy and appealing, said, "You might as well open your eyes, woman. It will get no better."

She only opened one.

But then she opened the other and felt her breath catch.

"Oh, fuck," she whispered. She rarely swore. But why let that stop her? She had gone and sent herself straight into hell.

"I'm in hell, aren't I?" she asked weakly, staring at the creature across from her.

Granted, he wasn't red.

And he didn't exude menace or evil.

But Lucifer wasn't supposed to…was he?

The creature laughed, a low, rolling sound that made her groin clench and throb. "No. You are not in hell. You may disagree, for a time. But hell, this is not." He started to cross the floor, but halted as her eyes widened.

"If I'm not in hell, then why am I looking at the devil?" she whispered before she could stop herself.

The creature—no, the man, for whatever he may be, he was most certainly still a man—arched a brow at her. A slow, sardonic smile touched his lips as he lifted one hand and stroked a finger over the ivory curve of one of the two horns gracing his skull. "Devil, no," he said. "Is your devil not said to be lovely and handsome, able to make you think he looks exactly the way he wants you to see him?" He flicked his hand toward his lower half and Pepper saw that his legs were indeed furred. Covered with a fine pelt of black fur from his navel down, his lower legs curved just a bit at the ankles, and ended into cloven hooves, exactly likely the 'devil' pictures. His muscled thighs looked like any man's, except the knees arched the wrong way, more like a goat's or a horse's.

Like the devil's.

Just like the devil pictures she had seen.

Well, not exactly…the fur tickled some memory.

Her eyes lingered briefly on the very human-looking cock that hung between his thighs before she jerked her eyes away and stared back into his exotic, dark eyes. He gave a slow, sexy smile and then moved away, out of her line of sight for a brief moment. When he reappeared, he had donned a loose-fitting pair of breeches that fell to just below his knees, rolled up in loose cuffs. She had an odd feeling he hated them, and wore them only because he knew his nudity bothered others.

"Do you think if I were your devil I would want to seem as such to you, sweet, pretty, lovely thing?" he purred, stalking closer, mesmerizing her, confusing her. He was breathtaking—

"What are you?" she asked shakily as he knelt beside her and cupped her face in one large palm.

He smiled, a curve of his full, sensual mouth that made her clench her thighs and stifle a moan. His skin was dusky, smooth, exuding the same scent that clung to the bed and bedclothes, and now her. His black hair, long and thick, straight and silky, fell over his wide, naked shoulder to tickle her flesh. It smelled the same, and left little trails of sensation everywhere it touched.

"A satyr," he purred, lowering his face until his pointed chin was propped on the bed and he was eye-to-eye with her, staring into her confused, bemused eyes…*oh, damn it, that face…I know that face. I've been dreaming of you*…she thought helplessly as he continued to stare at her, watching her with blank, black eyes.

A satyr.

"I'm not in hell," Pepper told him quietly, her voice a conspiratorial whisper. "I've lost my damn mind."

* * * * *

It wasn't an unusual response. Not for the adults who tumbled through the Gate. Arys smiled at her, revealing white, wickedly sharp teeth, his swarthy, lean face lighting with his smile, transforming with it. "I am not surprised, no, to hear you say," he said slowly, forcing the unusual words over his tongue while he studied her. He was going to have to touch her.

And he really did not want to do so.

Touching her meant he was going to feel her again, not just her soft skin, but her thoughts, her emotions, while he convinced her that she was in a real place. Mythe wasn't something she'd dreamed, or some make-believe world she had entered. He could not just block such things, it wasn't possible. The magick in his blood wouldn't allow him to convince her how very real Mythe was, but still allow him to keep himself separate from her.

And at the same time…his hands itched to touch her again. To move over that sweet mortal body, to taste her. His cock throbbed underneath the garment he had donned. *Get it over and done, Arys,* he told himself.

He laid the pads of his fingers lightly on her cheek and dove into her mind. *Satyr.* She was familiar with the word.

She was full of bright, burning energy, knowledge, a pure silvery, shining magick. She may not have opened the Gate this day, but she would have been able to eventually. Curiosity and wonder and love and faith, heaven above, she was almost like a child with all the awe he felt inside her.

Arys felt something inside her he hadn't expected to find. A very, *very* strong sexual pull, toward *him*.

And disappointment, all centered—

Oh, for the love of the unicorn, spare me. Disgust and irritation shuddered through Arys as pictures and images flitted through her mind, all within a few brief moments while he stared into her odd eyes, one was green, one was blue. Pictures she had seen in different places, but pictures of satyrs in very unlikely scenarios—because the satyrs were all *men* and they were only fucking *each* other. Not that it didn't happen, but it wasn't the norm. Satyrs were generally drawn to females, be they satyr, elf, human, vampire, or dryad. But the satyr male tended to prefer the female, contrary to what this female had learned in the mortal realm.

And now a new picture...she was trying to imagine him in those pictures.

Revulsion rolled through Arys. He had no qualms if others like him chose such pastimes. But not for him. His long dormant libido flared to sudden and rampant life. He certainly didn't want this sweet thing thinking...

"Not bloody likely, lass," he whispered roughly, moving his hand, sweeping his fingers down along her cheek, across her jaw until he could bury his fingers inside the fire of her hair, cupping her head and forcing her gaze to meet his. "You mortals and your damn misconceptions. Let us see if we cannot fix at least this one."

And then he lowered his head and covered her berry-pink mouth with his, pushing past the barrier of her lips and teeth with his tongue while she gasped in shock. He swung onto the bed, jerking the sheets down, pulling her lower body into close contact with his muscled thighs and rubbing his cock against her as he swept his tongue across hers, stroked her palate, tasted her. Her mouth widened greedily under his and Arys plundered deep, drinking in the taste of sweet, warm female.

He rolled atop her slim form and wedged his thighs between hers, rocking his thick, aching cock against her cleft while she moaned and whimpered underneath him, and the ridiculous pictures in her mind faded into nothingness. Once she was focused on him, and nothing else, he slid one long-fingered palm up her side and closed it over her breast, pinching the diamond-hard peak and rolling it as he sucked her tongue into his mouth and bit down.

He had never touched a mortal so—hadn't ever really wanted to. He'd been with faeries before, other satyr females, elves, a few vampire ladies, but never a human. Damnation, heaven and hell, she tasted so sweet, innocent and hot. He groaned, low and rough and pulled his mouth from hers to kiss his way down her throat, biting her skin gently over her throbbing pulse as he worked his way down her body to settle at her breasts.

"Only the body of a woman excites me, sweet," he murmured, staring at her full round breasts, the puckered, reddened nipples, the light-blue tracery of veins just beneath the surface of her pale satiny skin. "The way they smell, and look, and taste…" Lowering his head, he closed his mouth over one stiff peak and drew it deep, reveling in the weak moans that fell from her lips as her fingers threaded through his hair and fisted, holding him tightly against her.

He moved from one to the other, until both were gleaming wet, swollen and red from his mouth. Then he stared at her from under his lashes as he trailed the tips of his fingers across her slightly curved belly, his nails raking her flesh lightly as they glided toward her mound. "Why ever would I want to touch a satyr male?" he asked softly, lifting a brow at her. "If it is a cock I want to feel, I have one of my own...but this..."he slid his hand lower and without pause, plunged two long fingers inside her, shuddering as her silken, sweet flesh closed over him.

"This is the closest to heaven any man can hope to come while he walks in the world," he growled, pumping his wrist, grinning hotly as she started to rock her hips up against him, staring at him with dazed, bewildered eyes. "Sweet, tight, wet—the body of a woman gives us this. Bloody hell, I have to—"

She cried out as he moved suddenly and wedged his wide shoulders between her thighs, burying his face against her mound and driving his tongue deep inside her. Her taste, sharp and sweet, flooded his mouth as her hands tangled in his hair, grazing his horns with a feather light touch. He waited for her to shriek and jerk away but all she did was thrust her hips harder against him and moan wildly as he stabbed at her clit with his tongue.

He caught it between his teeth and tugged gently as he pushed his fingers back inside her snug little sheath. His cock throbbed and burned against his belly. Arys was aching to climb up her body and mount her, ride her until she exploded around him...it had been far too long—

She exploded even as he was thinking it, into his mouth, against his hands, her body tensing, her sheath spasming around his plunging fingers, cream soaking his hand, his face, as he greedily lapped it from her sex before propping himself up and staring at her broodingly.

He had a human in his bed.

And he really didn't know what to do about it.

* * * * *

Pepper forced her lids to lift. It wasn't easy. All she wanted to do was curl up and purr like a cat. The proverbial cat that ate the canary.

Of course, the problem was...she was the one who had just been eaten, and fairly well, not that she was much of a judge. Looking down over the length of her very naked body, she stared into the large, dark, slanted eyes of the man who called himself a satyr. And she blushed...not just from what he had done.

But what he had known.

He could obviously see inside her head.

He had seen the images she associated with satyrs. It was all she had ever picked up...randy, basically immoral, generally homosexual creatures that were half men, half goat who liked to rape unsuspecting trespassers and play tricks on the unwary. How degrading...

And this exotic creature was anything but that. Everything about him was beautiful, though she doubted he would have agreed with her. His face was a cross between handsome and beautiful, but thoroughly masculine, all planes and angles, except for that wide, full-lipped, sexy mouth that was even now wet from her, and set in unsmiling lines. His lips were dark, deep-toned rose, set beautifully in his swarthy face, with lean slashes in his

180

cheeks. His chin was triangular and should have looked odd, but it just looked…right.

His eyes were large and slanted, so black the pupil wasn't discernible. Feathery, dark winged brows and thick, silky black hair that fell far past his shoulders. His ears resembled what she would have expected an elf's to look like, long and pointed, curving through his thick, shining black hair. The two horns, white as his teeth and spiraling up from his skull, should have disturbed her.

They did not.

Why didn't they?

Neither did the silken fur she could feel against her calves and ankles as she shifted in the bed. He had cloven feet, and that didn't bother her either. None of it did. The musky scent that had first filled her head came from him, and it was delicious and all she wanted to do was taste him now, and see if she could…

A flush turned her cheeks pink as his eyes narrowed and she realized he was following the trail of her thoughts. His mouth curled up in a shadow of a smile and his fathomless eyes filled with heat. "Do you have to do that?"

"*Non.*"

French?

Then he frowned, shook his head, and said, "Not. No. I do not. But it is fun, such fun." Lowering his head, still watching her frown under his lashes, he licked her thigh, bit down just hard enough for her to feel the sting from his sharp teeth, then he soothed the sting away with his tongue. "Sweet, sweet thing," he murmured. "Long it has been since I've wanted a woman. A human? Never."

Her eyes narrowed and she hissed, "Wait a damn minute. Since you wanted a woman? You just said—"

He smiled, slowly, sadly. "Wanted no woman. Wanted no thing. Wanted nobody. My woman, she died. With my babe." He lowered his face back to her and breathed deeply, shuddering. It seemed to Pepper as if her scent was something that intoxicated him. "Until today. But I have always taken my pleasure with a woman, sweet. And I wish to take more."

Pepper blushed and then she whimpered as he used his tongue to part the lips of her sex again. She fisted her hands in his hair, one hand just above one of his curved, elongated ears. The other was fisted just at the base of one of his horns as she rocked her hips up, forcing her pussy closer and harder against his mouth as he sucked on her clit.

She moaned as he worked two fingers inside her cream-slicked sheath and started to pump, slowly and steadily, until she was eagerly riding his hand. He tore his mouth away from her, low melodious, foreign words falling from his mouth, sounding like music, but she suspected he was swearing instead as he moved atop her.

"Inside you," he rasped against her neck. "You do not know me, or this place. But I want to fuck you, and I want it now. Tell me yes, or tell me no, but tell me now, do it, before I lose my control, I do."

She was hungry, mindless, and dying inside. "Yes," she moaned.

He growled against her neck and she felt his hands as he tore away the drawstring from his pants and shoved aside the loose fitting garment, kicking it away. She threw her head back as he bit down at the spot where her neck and shoulder joined, a hungry growl falling from his lips as his elegant, long-fingered hands caught her thighs and opened them wide, his furred, muscled thighs holding hers open as he took his thick cock in hand and pressed it against her.

Closing his lips around the peak of one turgid nipple, he suckled deep before pulling away and murmuring, "Sweet, sweet, sweet," as he surged slowly inside, gritting his teeth as her satin-slicked muscles squeezed down around him. "Hmmm, shhh, relax, pretty one. Tight..."

Pepper gasped and shuddered when he scraped his nails across her clit, teasing her, beguiling her into relaxing for him. She tried, but he was so damn big... She flinched, a burning pain lancing through her vagina as he pushed his cock deeper inside her, tears stinging her eyes.

His exotic, dark eyes narrowed and he pushed up, the muscles in one arm bulging as he supported his weight on one hand while he caught her face and stared into her mismatched eyes, staring deep into her mind and soul... "Ahhh, damn me into the lowest corner of hell, I've got a sweet little human virgin in my bed."

His wide chest crushed her into the bed as he lowered himself atop her, taking some of the weight off his hips, so that his cock wasn't pushing so heavily into her. Then he started to rock slowly against her, pressing butterfly kisses onto her face, her nose, her mouth. Pulling out slowly, working his sex back in with lingering, gentle thrusts — just a little — before retreating. Reaching down to cup her hip in one hand, he nuzzled her chin, her neck and her mouth. Staring down into her eyes he whispered, "Soft, sweet little thing. So wet, so tight, so perfect."

Pepper stared up into his black eyes, half-terrified as the burning pain intensified. There was something beyond it, she could feel it, like when she had been able to feel *him* just beyond the cloudy wall that had obscured him from her, but she was unable to focus on it. His mouth covered hers roughly as he pulled his hips away, his thick cock rasping against her swollen, sensitive vagina.

His hand, hot, firm, calloused, stroked its way up from her hip to her breast, cupping and stroking the smooth, plump flesh there, rolling the nipple, milking it.

Hmmm, that was rather...nice.

His tongue pushed inside her mouth, bringing his taste, something unique and male and appetizing. She wrapped her arms hungrily around his neck, forgetting the head of his cock, lodged just at her entrance.

And then he drove deep inside, completely, slicing through her virgin passage and burying his cock completely, until his sac rested against the cleft of her bottom and she was staring up at him with tear-drenched eyes, her mouth trembling, her sex aching and burning. He whispered roughly against her mouth, "Sorry, so sorry, am I, sweet, sweet thing. Pretty girl, pretty mine. Over is it...yes? Pleasure I give, *non*? Hmmm, so sweet...tight...so hot."

His voice, hot, dark, sweet, like candy, rolled over her, soothed her, aroused her, all at the same time, while he cupped one hip in his hand and stroked it, holding still inside her pussy, his cock jerking and twitching hungrily. His heart pounded heavily against her chest, echoing her own.

When all she did was stare up at him, afraid to move, afraid to blink, he smiled, a hot lazy curl of his lips, and promised roughly, "No pain, this. Just the pleasure from now on." And he started to pump his hips, cupping her head in his hands and covering her mouth with his, sucking her tongue inside his mouth, inviting her to taste and play, like he had done to her. Pepper gasped as hot little licks of pleasure arced through her with each thrust of his cock inside her, as the thick, rounded head stroked over a sensitive spot buried deep within her.

Against her inner thighs, she could feel the silken caress of his furred, muscled thighs and she shuddered. His scent, that intoxicating, sensual scent filled her head, her mouth until it was there with every breath she took, making her lungs burn, making her crave more and more as he surged slowly back inside.

A weak, mewling whimper started to echo through the room. Her? She didn't care. She eagerly drove her tongue into his mouth, seeking his taste, and she felt his wide chest shudder as he groaned in pleasure. He pushed deeper, harder inside her and she sobbed, her head falling back. His lips moved down her chin to her neck, and he chuckled as she moaned when he closed them over her nipple. One hand clasped her thigh and pushed it high, opening her, leaving her exposed as he pushed deep, his pelt stroking silkily over her thighs, his groin caressing her mound as he drove deep.

Arys swiveled his hips, using his body to stroke her clit and she shuddered. He did it a second time, then a third and she shrieked. Sliding his hand between them, he stroked his thumb over the engorged little bud, then pushed down and watched as she went screaming into climax.

It tightened, swelled, broke over her like waves breaking over the sand, and she fell back against the sheets. There was still an edgy, needy yearning in her belly and she reached hungrily for him as he surged inside her, the clinging, wet muscles of her sheath holding snug to his cock as he drove back into her, quick and hard.

Pepper tensed as he started to pound heavily into her, felt the promise of pain, but she didn't really care as long as this wonderful, incredible man kept stroking her clit, as long he kept touching her, as long he kept suckling on her nipples and looking at her through his ridiculously long lashes like he thought she was so amazingly sexy and beautiful...oh.

"Please...again, please," she sobbed as she felt something tightening inside her again as he continued to ride her hard and fast.

He growled against her flesh, released her nipple with a wet little pop and moved up on her body, murmuring in a deep rasp, "Such a hungry pretty you are." Then he framed her face in his dark, long-fingered hands, kissing her roughly as he started to fill her with deep, long, slow strokes that had her arching her hips against his.

With near bruising force, he drove deep inside and Pepper screamed, her choking cry dying in his mouth as he swallowed it down. His hand tangled tightly in her hair, his hips pounded against hers, and the room filled with the sounds of deep, hungry moans and gasping sighs, the sounds of good, hard sex.

When she came this time, he came with her, in hot, wet pulsing jets, with a muffled roar against her neck, while she screamed and raked her nails across his shoulders. Her vagina clamped down around his jerking cock, squeezing and milking him until he emptied himself and collapsed atop her with a moan, wrapping his lean, muscled arms around her and rolling until she lay on top of him.

He murmured to her, his words musical, sweet, concerned. Foreign. And questioning. She lifted her gaze to his, unable to summon the energy to actually move.

"Huh?" was about all the intelligent thinking she could manage.

He chuckled and closed his eyes. "Are you...well, pretty one? Hurt you, did I?" he asked, stroking one hand down her back, lingering on her bottom.

"Hmmm. A little. I'm fine. Tired. Sleepy." Then she closed her eyes and snuggled up against him.

"Your name...first," he whispered against her hair. "Bad enough, it is, I've seduced you and have had my wicked, wicked way with you—" he was grinning against her hair, she could feel it. "But we shouldn't tumble into dreams without at least knowing our names? Arys, I am called."

She smiled, stroked her hand down his sleek, smoothly muscled chest. "Pepper. I'm called Pepper. I'm really not dreaming, am I?"

He sighed. "*Non.* No. No dreaming. Sleep, pretty little Pepper. I will explain what I can. When you waken."

She couldn't fight such logic, not when delivered in such a sexy voice. She closed her eyes and slid into sleep even as he was tugging a blanket over her, one that was warm, and smelled of him. *Arys,* his name was.

Arys.

* * * * *

Arys was a bloody bastard.

Arys was selfish.

Arys was a moron.

Arys was a lecher.

Arys couldn't stop grinning. He stroked his hands down the smooth warm expanse of her naked back and wondered how long it had been since he had felt so *content*. Weeks. Months. Years? He missed Lorne, mourned her. Had loved her, in a companionable way, had lusted after her, truly.

But had he ever felt like this after mating with her? He did not think so. Resting his hand right above Pepper's smooth, delightfully round little ass, he pondered it. And the smile that stretched his face. No. Long had it been since he had felt so happy after a fucking.

Pepper. What an odd name.

His knack for languages of the mortal realm told him it was something they used to spice their foods, like gnomes used, similar to *kiar*, spicy and hot. He glanced at her hair and wondered if that was why.

But his mind was heavy with exhaustion, and the need to rest. He had explanations to make upon the human's waking—and she was quick-witted, so he'd best have all his wits about him as well. Not that he was likely to be able to do that. Every time he would look at her, from now until the world stopped spinning, he would remember how she felt, with her sweet sheath wrapped snug around his cock, how she tasted, how she moaned...

* * * * *

Pepper woke with a moan on her lips, and his mouth on her sex. His hands, those elegant, masculinely beautiful hands, gripped her hips as soon as he saw her eyes flutter open. Taking his mouth away from her sex he pulled her to the edge of the bed and flipped her onto her belly, urging her to her feet and bending her over.

Arys stared hungrily down the sweet curve of her rump as he pushed his dark cock into her sex, shuddering as her wet, swollen tissues closed tightly around him, the fat head of his cock rasping against the bundle of nerves deep inside her passage as he buried himself completely inside her. Her body trembled around him and he stroked his hands over the globes of her ass, the curve of her hips as he murmured reassuringly in his own tongue and started to thrust deep. His balls were already drawn tight against him, and his cock felt as though it were on fire as he thrust inside the silken wet well of her pussy.

She whimpered and pushed back at him, sobbing out his name. Bracing his knees, gripping her hips tightly, he drove harder and harder inside her, shuddering as her cries echoed through the *iskita*. The muscles in her vagina started to convulse and clamp down around him.

Arys used his weight to ride her down, pinning her between the bed and his body, wrapping one muscled arm around her slender torso, and cupping a plump breast in his hand, tweaking the nipple. He set his teeth in her shoulder and bit down as he drove his hips higher and higher, harder and harder into her, as her sweet little pussy clung wetly to him, as though trying to keep his cock inside her.

Pepper's head fell back against his shoulder and she started to scream as her orgasm began, starting with slow, delicious little milking sensations that built and built until she was locking down on Arys' cock to the point of near pain. He jackhammered his cock into her and flooded her with hot, wet jets of semen and she milked him, drawing it on and on, until she had drained him, totally emptied him. And left him feeling more complete than he had ever felt in his life.

He slumped forward, his hair tangling with hers, his horns on the mattress as they gasped and struggled to breathe. In his own tongue, he whispered, "The unicorn said you were coming, and you were coming for me. Please, do not ask me to let you go."

Chapter Four

Pepper sat neck deep in a warm pool of mineral water that soothed her muscles and bubbled and frothed around her better than even the finest Jacuzzi. Arys sat across from her, dangling his legs in the pool, watching her somberly. "No bath?" she asked, feeling a little nervous under his intense scrutiny.

"Not as sore as you, am I," he said in his slow, lyrical way, shaking his head. His black hair slid over his shoulder as he did so, his slender, slightly spiraling horns catching and reflecting the dappled sunlight. "I bathed in my *iskita* while resting you were."

She smiled slowly. "I love your voice, the way you talk," she said suddenly, her cheeks flushing pink. "Of course, you probably already know that."

He grinned slightly. "*Non.*" He frowned, shook his head. "No. Only touching you. I need to be touching you, thinking of you to see your thoughts." A wolfish grin slashed across his face and he added, "Touching you evermore will be making thinking difficult, I fear. Sweet, hot little thing…"

Pepper swallowed, her mouth suddenly dry. Hadn't the water been warm a few minutes ago, a few seconds ago? Why did it suddenly feel so cool? Staring into his slanted, blacker than black eyes, she felt as through she were falling, drowning, flying all at the same time. His lids lowered, his lashes veiling his eyes and she felt as through a spell had been broken. "You need your rest, pretty mine," he said roughly, his wide shoulders lifting in a sigh. "And talking, we must be. You are wanting to know what is…going on?"

Going along with his obvious attempts to guide the conversation to safer topics, she decided to have a question answered. "How do you know English?" she asked. "French? Are those the languages spoken here?"

"Several of your tongues, I know. English, as you say. French, Spanish, some Deutsch. A bit of Portuguese. The Gate opens to places where these tongues are spoken. I have a…talent for languages, so easy it was to learn when a refugee came through the Gate. Some who speak like you, though not well, I fear. The words tangle my tongue. And many who speak French." His eyes got a bit distant and he didn't seem to seeing anything. "Lorne…my woman, she wished — *non*…no reason to…how feel you?"

Pepper frowned. What had he been going to say? Lorne? His woman. The one who had died. He was so sad. But something inside her said that wasn't his normal state. There was laughter, love, and light locked inside him. Forcing her melancholy away, she fluttered her lashes at him and teased, "I'm not sure. Should you come and feel me and see?"

His eyes heated and a reluctant grin crept across his face. "Minx is what you are," he said, shaking his head again. "Devil woman." He took something from his side and rose, coming around the pool and sitting behind her. "Clean you up. Before you tempt me beyond all reason." One hand slid down her wet shoulder and closed over her breast, rolling her nipple into a tight, hard bud while he lowered his head and whispered darkly, "Many things I wish to do, and show, to you. If you are still wanting me, after we talk, then we will be starting. I promise you that, sweet Pepper."

A few moments later, she was sighing in pleasure as strong hands massaged her scalp and washed her thick, heavy curls. *Forget the hair salons when you get back home, Pepper. They will never measure up to this,* she thought as his hands urged her to slide forward and lean back so he could rinse her hair.

She frowned slightly at the odd little sensation low in her belly as she thought of home.

Going home would mean...*leaving Arys.*

* * * * *

She watched nervously as he prowled the house. No, is-something or other. Is...is...iskita. *Iskita.* That was what he had called it. She wore something of his, a long flowing white shirt that fell to her knees. It was practically transparent and probably not worn much, because his scent clung to it only faintly, but since she didn't have any clothes...and besides, it was *his.*

Something was bothering him.

"Out with it, Arys," she finally said, fidgeting a little with the flowing lace on one of the cuffs. Then she shoved her hair out of her face and met his eyes when he stopped pacing and turned to stare at her broodingly, crossing his arms over his chest. He had donned some clothing, of a sort. Loose breeches, held around his waist by a drawstring. It hid the pelt of hair that started right below his navel. She felt a fine tremble run through her as she recalled how those strong, muscled legs, that silken hair had felt against her last night and this morning as he had loved her. And it had felt like loving, not like, well, just sex.

Of course, she hadn't ever done it before, so maybe she was just confusing the two.

Damn it, but she loved looking at him. His sable hair fell halfway down his back, in straight, silky tresses that she had buried and tangled her hands in only hours ago. It spilled over shoulders wide and strong and proud, sculpted with firm, delineated muscles, as were his arms and his chest. His skin was a swarthy, coppery gold, and a lean, flat belly tapered down to his hips and groin where the fine dark pelt of fur started. His hips, narrow and slim, his ass, and his legs, save for the pelt of hair, were exactly like a human's — perfectly formed — until right at his knee, when they curved back and arched, then down into the cloven foot.

Long, lean, and perfect, just looking at him made her heart hurt, and her body ache, itching to touch.

"Does what you see disturb you?" he asked, his voice soft, silky, menacing.

She shook herself, realizing she had been staring at him. Again. Lifting her eyes, she smiled softly, and said, "No. What I see fascinates me, seduces me, and enthralls me. You're the most beautiful man I've ever seen in my life."

That seemed to take him aback a little. A frown turned his mouth down.

"You don't smile enough, satyr," she said softly, walking across the distance that separated them and pressing her finger to his mouth. "So serious. Have you always been so serious?"

"*Non.* Not always serious," he said slowly, grasping her wrist. Staring into her eyes, he slid her finger into the hot, wet cave of his mouth and sucked it, stroking it with his tongue, then withdrawing it in a slow, subtle caress. "But laughter has been gone from me, long has it been gone."

When he released her hand, Pepper spread them both in front of her and formed a glittery, silvery ball of light, pleased that even though she was not in her world, the magick was still there. "Do you know I was a baby when I first found my magick? It was bad, though. Very bad. I first tried this when I was five, in front of my parents." The ball grew bigger and bigger, and as it did, Arys realized there was water inside, or the illusion of it.

And the illusion of fish.

"They wouldn't let me have a pet. Said I needed to be a little bigger and understand responsibility. So I told them I was a witch, and I could make my own, and it would be the biggest and bestest fish bowl in all the world—"

And the results were, as she planned, exactly the same now as they had been twenty years ago. The silvery fish 'ball' exploded, the illusory water spilling out and the power of her illusion making them both appear to be wet and soaked, the sheerness of her shirt making her look as though she wore nothing. The 'fish' faded away to nothing, because the trauma of watching her 'pets' die had hurt, even though her mother had assured her they weren't real.

A deep, rough, startled chuckle escaped Arys' lips without him realizing it as the fish 'ball' broke over them. She gave him a mock pout, even though hearing him laugh made her want to dance. "Oh, go ahead and laugh about it. You've no idea how frustrating it was, being such a talented, awkward little witch. Mama and Daddy were at their wits end trying to deal with me. When I was eight, I decided I wanted a pony..."

He smiled as he moved closer and cupped her breasts through her 'wet' shirt. "You are trying to distract me, pretty mine," he murmured, rocking his hips against her belly, sliding his hands down and around to cup her butt and lift her against him.

Smiling flirtatiously, she said, "Did it work?" as the 'water' just dried away from them, leaving her shirt as opaque as it was going to get. She stared up into his eyes, reaching up to cup his cheek. "You've got sad eyes. I don't like seeing anybody sad. But it hurts my heart to see you sad. Why is that? Yesterday morning, I didn't even know you, didn't know anything about this place..."

His mouth cut off her words as he kissed her hungrily, almost desperately, his fingers biting into her ass as he lifted her up, one arm under her buttocks bracing her weight, the other hand burying itself in her damp hair.

She was suddenly adrift when he set her on her feet and stalked away.

"You fell through the Gate. You were using your magick, trying to open it. Succeeded, you would have, and soon. Such power you have inside you," he said, biting the words off as though they hurt his throat. He stood across the room, his hands at his sides, curled into loose fists. "The Gate is mine to watch. A...friend sensed a disturbance and we went to see. We saw you.

"The Gates open to allow refugees, we call them — those who are hurt, desperate, or in danger — to enter our world from yours. Usually children who are gifted, like you, and who are treated harshly or cruelly by their kin. Battered, abused women find the Gates as well. Sometimes those who fall into the death-sleep fall through the Gates. We do not understand them completely, no, we do not.

"Guard them, we must. Some strong black magick workers can use the blood of the Gate watchers to force it open and slip through from our realm into yours. But such an act causes pain and death in our world, and disasters in yours, disruptions in your nature. Those who try, we kill. The Gate opens when it chooses — we do not allow it to be opened by force."

With those final words, he jutted his chin out at her.

Daring her to speak.

"So basically, you're telling me I'm stuck here."

Chapter Five

Arys watched as she slid through the door, watched as she walked to the stream and settled at the edge, her face somber and serious. *Handled that well, didn't I?*

A familiar, gentle touch on his mind and he glanced out the window and saw a shining white-and-gray form. Faryn whickered softly. *I smell a woman, and sex.*

Go away, meddlesome unicorn.

Is that any way to talk to somebody who is trying to help you attain what you desire most?

What I desire most is to stop this infernal hurting —

You were hurting even when you were with Lorne. She kept you warm at night, but she was not your true mate. I pity you the loss of your babe, truly I do, Arys. But while Lorne did love you, she did not accept what you are, she was not a helpmate. This one will be. He nodded his head toward the stream. *And more than a helpmate, truly. She has the heart of a warrior. A heart like your own. Arys, we have trouble coming. We feel like it, in our hearts. The Watchers feel a darkness in the world. You are bound to the earth. Do not tell me you have not felt it.*

"You expect me to believe that sweet, pretty little thing is a warrior witch?" Arys scoffed, shaking his head. "Fool's dreams, you are telling me. She's like a faerie, making rainbows dance and..."

Forgotten your history, have you? Remember the Legion Wars? The Faeries made the forest of Asmere run red with the blood of their enemies, Faryn said, his 'voice' dropping to a soft throb that lingered just behind Arys' eyes. *Even the meekest creature will turn into a demon if it is provoked. But she is not meek. She may look sweet, but she is no mild, easily cowed little mortal.*

No. Not easily cowed, not meek. She sat, shoulders straight, legs crossed, head back so that her hair billowed down her back in a banner of red curls, her eyes trained on the leaf-dappled sky. Her hands were clenched into small fists that she held in her lap.

She would never be going home.

Roughly, Arys said, "I did not handle it well, the telling. I...I handled it badly. Very badly. She could force the Gate to open if she wanted to. None of us here have the power to stop her. Daklin and the elves could keep her from trying, perhaps, with the power the enchanted kingdoms hold inside them. Ronal could hold her mind sway, but only if she were inside his lands, under his power. And either he or Cray could mayhap seduce her—" a growl trickled from Arys' throat before he could stop it and his nails bit into his hands as he fisted them, the veins bulging out in his forearms as fury raced through him.

"I have only the magick being the Gatekeeper gives me. And simple earth magick any satyr can call. But nothing that could bind hers and keep her from leaving, should she try. And I could never harm her."

She will not try. Faryn whickered and tossed his head. *Her own honor will stop her. Opening a Gate forcefully would not harm one, but many. She would never try to harm an innocent, and she believes you. She may well question you further, but she believes you.* Amusement flowed from the 'corn's eyes as the stallion slid Arys a narrow look. *And besides...neither an angel, fallen or otherwise, nor a vampire are any better at seduction than a satyr, no matter what the tales may say. She is already enthralled with you, and well you know it.*

Enthralled? Arys slid the 'corn a wry glance and muttered, "Not bloody likely. When she meets the other Pillars, then we will see enthrallment. Right now, she's enjoying her first bit o' sex. When she sees the fallen black angel, or when Ronal lays his eyes on her and decides he wants to see if she's a tasty bit, or when the elf wants to take her to the elf kingdoms for magick training, then we shall be seeing enthrallment, and she'll give me nary a glance."

And the jealousy was already eating a hole in his gut.

Whirling, he stomped across the *iskita* and slammed his fist into the wall, then rested his forehead against the wall as he pulled his fist through the shattered wood, dark violet blood trickling down his swarthy skin. "I will never have her, Faryn, and I want her so badly," he whispered to the fae creature just outside.

Faryn's answer was merely a soft, comforting whicker, and then he was gone, his silvery hooves silent on the floor of the Satyr's Wood. Closing his eyes, Arys said softly, to whoever might be listening, "You should not have given her to me, not for just a while. If I cannot keep her, then this is just cruel."

He heard a familiar chiming and turned to see the black mirror on the opposite wall gleaming. He crossed to it and moved his marked hand over it, sighing as he did so. He had little patience for politics now but something told him he was going to have to handle them. The opaque blackness of the mirror cleared and he met Daklin's eyes, clear and blue as the summer sky, set in an ivory-pale face. His familiar, handsome face was lit with amusement and his eyes were glowing with it.

"You are in such trouble, my friend," Daklin said, his voice lilting and musical. His silvery-blond brows peaked and he clucked his tongue. "The Council doesn't take well to their orders being ignored."

"Tell that to the Gates. I have no control over when they choose to open—tell that to the bloody Council," Arys said, plowing a long-fingered hand through his hair, unaware of how agitated he looked to his longtime friend.

Daklin's eyes widened. "A refugee? A child? Do not tell me we have another broken, wounded one to heal, Arys, please. My heart canna handle another so soon," he begged, recalling the last child, a tiny girl of only five. Her father—no, he was not going to think of that. Her father had gotten his just reward, not what he deserved, no punishment was great enough. But he had reaped what he sowed. Even though they couldn't cross the Gates, magick *could* cross them…and did.

"No. Not a refugee. A…a witch," Arys said slowly, turning to stare out the window. Pepper was just barely visible from this angle, her head bent low as she stared into the water, her expression pensive. *What is she thinking?*

"A witch? From the mortal realms? Did she open the Gates?" Daklin asked, moving closer and craning his neck. He couldn't cross the mirror, but he could damn well *see.* His blue eyes narrowed as he caught sight of the female and …how very little she wore. "Hmmm, do tell," he purred in elvish.

"Nay, she did not open the Gate. The Gate opened for her," he said quietly. "I believe in time, she could have opened it. But it opened for her."

"Why? Is she in trouble? Is she needed?"

"Trouble? No."

"Needed?" Daklin persisted.

"Aye," Arys said, reaching up and absently stroking one horn. "Needed, aye."

"For what?" Daklin said, rolling his eyes. The satyr was usually not so…reticent.

Arys turned slowly and lifted his troubled eyes to meet the elf's. "Needed for me, I think. The unicorn Faryn says she is here for *me*."

Daklin looked stunned. Briefly. Very briefly. Very little made an elf pause. Then slowly, a wide, wide smile curled his mouth. "Then why in the name of all the Hells are you looking so grim? By this elf's eyesight, which is pretty sharp, might I add, she looks…delicious."

Arys gave Daklin a narrow look. "Why in the fuck would a human wish to mate for life with a bloody satyr?"

Daklin lifted one brow. "And why, by the Father and the Heavens, would she be brought here, *for you*, if she wasn't likely to do just that?" the elf replied easily. He nodded in the direction of the stream. "She is done with her pondering, I believe."

"You're a satyr, Arys, as you were always meant to be. That is not a bloody monster. You are a good and true friend, a good man. By the blood, man, a satyr is sex incarnate, not a demon, a troll, or mongrel whelp—do not listen to what some small-minded bigots still believe. You are known as friend among the elves and humans and the watchers. That should count as more than what bigots believe."

Daklin touched his fingers to the mirror from his rooms at the Council, and the mirror blackened once more, just as Arys heard Pepper moving toward the door.

"Did I hear voices, besides yours I mean?" she asked quietly, poised at the threshold.

"*Oui*…yes. A friend," he said, gesturing to the mirror. "We…ahh…speak through the mirror."

"*Through the Looking Glass*," she said with an odd little smile. "Now I really feel like Alice. I just need a blue dress and a white apron."

"I will find some clothes—"

"I was being a smart-ass. It's a book from home about a girl who falls through a mirror into another world, or something like that. I read it a long time ago," she said, moving closer and peering at the mirror with curious eyes. "I can't say I'm happy about this. There are things at home that are important. Friends I will miss. I'm mad. I can't lie about that. And I want to throw a temper tantrum but odd things happen when I do that. So I'd appreciate you showing me a safe place where I can have at it."

When he looked, really looked, he could see the gleam of temper well-hidden in her two-colored eyes. Her cheeks were high with color, and her eyes were snapping with it.

"I…I sense there is something else…?"

"Yes. A but. There was a 'but'. Going back—even before you told me I couldn't—going back meant something that made me feel a little sick inside. I didn't like the thought of never seeing you again," she said looking at him squarely, lifting her chin. "I *hated* the thought of never seeing you again. I don't even know you. How can I already feel that way?"

Arys couldn't answer. He had already backed her up against the wall and, with a groan he grabbed her around the waist, covering her mouth with his, thrusting his tongue into the sweet well, gathering her taste and reveling in it as his strong agile hands ripped the shirt from her lovely little body.

Pepper gasped with shock as she felt him lift her and pierce her, driving his cock home even as his hands were spreading her thighs, lifting them, guiding them around his waist as his cock forged through the tight, swollen tissues of her pussy.

The silken pelt of his lower body caressed her thighs, driving his thick length inside as he pushed home again, and again, while his mouth ate hungrily at hers.

His cock pulsed inside her, throbbed and swelled as his head lifted and his eyes met hers. "Say it, Pepper. Pretty mine. Again, will you tell me? That you do not wish to leave?"

Gasping for air, she whimpered, "I *can't* leave. You're part of me."

She felt her control slipping. On her temper. And her magick. Hot licks of lust flooded her, and little bursts of power were starting to leak. Plumes of smoke and mist filled the room. Rainbows danced around the ceiling. And the floor trembled. His mouth left hers and he moved down her neck, biting and licking as he went and driving his cock high and hard, the thick, rounded head rasping over the nerve bed high inside her pussy.

Fire…the heat of it flooded her magick senses and she dampened it, sent it into the fireplace. She heard the muffled roar of it and sobbed with frustration at not being able to lose control completely. Arys sensed something held in check and he growled in warning, setting his teeth into the curve between neck and shoulder, looping his arms under her knees, opening her wide, and pounding into her hard and furiously, sliding his swollen, throbbing length into the slick wet channel of her pussy as her head fell back and she screamed out his name.

Her control slipped, shattered, and she wailed, forcing the wild magick into something she hoped was relatively harmless, hearing the wild booming noises, familiar from childhood, as Arys thrust heavily inside her, his teeth marking her before he moved his mouth up to hers in a line of bruising, biting kisses that stung like fire along her sensitized flesh.

Mine...

Mine...

Mine...

She felt the alien caress on her mind and shook from the absolute possession, the absolute utter need she heard there. His body shifted against hers, and he dragged himself against her clit, his chest caressing the peaked flesh of her nipples and she broke as he rasped against her lips, "Mine..."And it was echoed inside of her...no matter how angry she might be about being uprooted from her home, her life—what life had she had there really? Looping her arms around his neck, she fiercely whispered back, "Mine."

She sobbed as the tightening in her womb overtook her and broke over her body, rhythmic pulsing sensations in her sheath milking his cock as he started to pump her full of his seed.

Smoke, sulphur, mist and rainbow lights filled the air around them as he opened his large, slanted eyes long moments later, slowly letting her slide her legs to the floor. In a gesture that was slowly coming to be familiar to her, she watched as he absently brushed his hair out of his eyes, and stroked one of his curved, slightly spiraled horns, studying the slowly fading, flickering lights.

"I thought...the earth moved. It truly did." A slow smile tugged at his mouth.

She sulked. "Told you I was mad. I can't control my temper and...hmmm, well."

An all-out grin lit his impossibly exotic face as he pulled out of her and moved just a few inches away. "Disappointed, am I. Wanted badly to make the earth seem to move for you," he said teasingly. "And here you go, making it well and truly move." A thoughtful look came over his face. "You make me as once I was. As I am meant to be."

"What do you mean?" she asked, reaching up, winding a strand of his hair around her finger, loving the silkiness of it.

A tiny grin returned to his mouth. "Playful. Happy. Somber does not become a satyr. I have felt no happiness for so long, I cannot remember. *Non.* Remember, I do not." Unwillingly, he cupped her face and said softly, "You will not wish to stay always with me, a satyr. We have many, many wonders in Mythe. Not one of them."

Pepper arched a brow. "I think you're wrong," she said, shrugging a round, naked shoulder. The scent of him clung to her, and intoxicated her. Everywhere he touched her made her burn and ache, and already she wanted him again. "I *know* you are, but that will take—"

A booming, shattering noise filled the air. "By the Blood," Arys snapped, jerking her against him and turning his back as the air seemed to shatter and split.

Pepper yelped instinctively, but another instinct surged to the fore and she tried to push away from Arys.

His body was powerful. Deceptively slim. Those wide shoulders should have warned her. He crushed her to his chest as she tried to push away and whispered reassuring, "Hush now, *amour*. Friends, they are. But they know you not."

Me, either, she thought, clenching her teeth, closing her eyes and loosing a bit of magick, thinking of *shields...stone...lightning...* Her eyes opened and when she looked, from what she could see with her face buried against Arys' firm, heavenly feeling chest, the faint otherworldly glow told her the shield was there. She could feel it, sense it. Nobody else was likely to. Until they tried to approach, of course.

Damn, I'm good, she thought smugly. Her beliefs had always been the scapegoat. Her magick was what separated her. She needed no incantations, no secret article or object. All she needed was herself.

Just beyond the barrier, a mist was forming, thickening, and inside it, something else was forming. Or someone else. Elses.

Two men. Both tall. Very tall.

And one had...*wings?*

The first one to step out...*oh, hell, I've fallen into Lord of the Rings.* He had silvery blond hair with two braids, one at each temple, eyes the color of the sky in winter — clear, cold blue — a handsome, poetically beautiful yet masculine face, a sculpted mouth. He was saved from being too beautiful by the humor and the mischief that danced in his eyes as he studied her, his head cocked to the side. His ears...high curved ears...were elf's ears, the curve of the right one pierced with a loop of gold. He caught sight of Arys and his eyes lit with amusement, pleasure and mischief as he moved clear of the mist, his every movement as graceful as a dancer's.

He moved closer to reach out to Arys, but his hand encountered the shield only Pepper's eyes could see and he bellowed as a white-hot bolt of electrical current shocked him painfully. He backpedaled, his hand held to his chest, his eyes narrowed, glaring at them both.

Arys glanced down at Pepper, who was smiling sweetly. He bent and snatched up the shirt he had pulled from her body and covered her with it as best he could. The buttons were missing, and one sleeve torn, but at least she was covered. "Friends, I said. Friends, they are," he said, shaking his head. He wasn't quite able to hide the grin on his face.

"Yours. I don't know them from Adam," she said, shaking her head, the tumbled red curls falling into her eyes. Tossing the curls out of her eyes, she said, "A woman has to protect herself."

Stroking one hand down her arm, he kissed her lightly, and murmured, "I protect what is mine."

She should have been insulted. She was fully capable of protecting herself. But it sent a thrill down her spine to hear him say that. She slid her eyes back to the men who were watching them with very intense interest. The blond *elf* was shaking his hand, and eyeing her warily as he scanned the area around them, most likely trying to pinpoint where the barrier lay.

"You can release the shielding," Arys whispered into her hair. "They are no threat. To allow it to remain may...insult...truly, these are friends. They mean you no harm, they bring no harm here. Closer to me than my own blood, and they would lay down their lives to protect what I hold dear."

She poked her lip out slightly and rolled her eyes but pulled the magick back inside her, watching as the elf's eyes widened in appreciation at the slow, subtle flexing of power the act took. "I trust you," she whispered back to Arys. "And that's the only reason I did that. I don't trust many."

Once more, the elf approached, slowly but confidently, his eyes fixed on her face. He spoke, and the words that fell from his hips were musical like bells, liquid and golden. Then he laughed when Arys replied back, in English, "'Tis rude to speak, Daklin, in a tongue that not all understand, and very well you know this."

"Pardon, then, I beg," the man said. "I speak not as well as the satyr. Well enough. Well enough. Daklin, my name is." He lifted his fingers to his lips, touched them briefly and then touched them to hers. "Greetings, I give you, lady of the mortal realms. A witch, you are? Welcome, here be you."

Pepper had to tip her head up to stare at him, considering he stood a good foot and a half taller, with wide, wide shoulders, a broad, deep chest that tapered down to a narrow waist with lean hips, muscled legs...*oh, yummy*, the thought took a brief trip through her mind, and then she settled back with a smile against Arys. Breathing in his scent, she let it fill her head and her lungs as she turned her eyes to the second newcomer. Magick was rumbling through the air and her skin was all but jumping with it, her eyelids twitching, throat tight.

And when she focused those eyes on this newcomer, she nearly swallowed her tongue. Wings. Yes...it had been wings she had seen in the mist, not some trick of light and mist and illusion.

True wings, pearl gray, silver, white, that rose behind his shoulders, the apex jutting just to the top of his head and the bottom of them coming to just above his ankles. Wings. She slid her eyes up the length of his thickly muscled thighs, exposed by the short, kiltlike garment he wore, over a carved abdomen, and a bare chest with powerful muscles...*the wings,* she wondered? His arms were corded and long, roped with sinewy muscle. She tore her gaze away from his body and met his eyes, deep fathomless pools of silvery, swirling-gray and silver, like his wings, full of magick and curiosity and mystery...and *pain...*

And then he blinked, drooping heavily-lashed lids over those fantastic eyes, and when he opened them, all that emotion, all that magick was gone. His golden skin was shades lighter than Arys' and as he moved, all those muscles rippled and flexed.

He glanced once at Arys, his eyes grim, his mouth somber. A thousand unspoken words seemed to pass between them and Pepper felt Arys' hands tighten around her waist, felt some odd pain coming from him. She snuggled more firmly against him and waited for this new being to speak.

"This is Cray," Arys finally said after a long silence passed.

Cray nodded at her and crossed one arm against his chest, bowing to her, the edges of his wings falling around him like a cloak. "Lady," he said quietly, his voice deep and low, husky. "Not who we expect to see through Gates." He straightened and studied her with deep, piercing eyes, almost...waiting.

She returned his stare, linking the fingers of one hand absently through the fingers that Arys had wrapped tightly around her waist. Cray's eyes, so like storm clouds, dropped and watched the gesture, and a small smile curved his mouth. He lifted his eyes up, following over the lines of her body. She felt the skin ruffling touch of magick, though she heard nothing more than a whisper in the air. Then Arys' body tightened and his mouth firmed out. His lips moved and his head shook in a slight negative. She could *hear* his voice, in the back of her head, but not his words.

"Ummm, excuse me, but if you're talking about me, I think I deserve to know what you're saying," she said as politely as she could, tapping her foot in annoyance, then narrowing her eyes as the three men turned bland looks in her direction. The *oh, I'm sorry, but what do you mean* look. And she wasn't fooled.

Cray was the first to smile. The smile spread upward from his mouth until his eyes sparkled with it. "No need to worry for you, Arys. She is completely yours. Understands you, and feels your mind touch already, she does," the winged man murmured, shaking his head. He moved closer, the smaller feathers along the edges of his wings ruffling with his movement. He stopped just in front of her and lifted a hand, the palm nearly as large as her face.

He was *massive…*Nearly seven feet tall, she imagined. His hair, raven wing black, and raining down past his shoulders, shone in the flickering light. "Not drawn to Daklin or me…nor will the vampire sway her. She is *yours*," Cray said, his eyes half-closed.

Pepper could feel him, half inside her mind, and it was a seductive touch, enticing, even though he didn't mean for it to be, and with an outraged cry she threw him out and bolted down her own mental shields. Her psychic skills weren't as powerful as her magicking ones, but she could bolster them with magick shields. "Stay out of my head," she rasped as she used her own bit of power to shove him away from her, calling up wind magick and forcing him back.

Cray's eyes widened as he felt her bar him from her mind, something most mortal women could not do, witch or not. The punch of wind, powerful but familiar against his chest was strong enough to force him back and he went, narrowing his eyes and studying her flushed face, the gleam of unwanted arousal, the anger. His physical presence had done little, but his touching her mind, just wanting to see how she already had pledged herself to his friend...

"An apology must be made, I believe. I trespassed. I had no right," Cray murmured, going to one knee, his wings spreading wide around him like a cloak, his head lowered. He could smell her, smell the satyr, the mingled scent of their sex...his cock swelled beneath his wrap and Cray ached and fought the urge to swear in frustration. This woman, this slim little red-headed witch from the mortal world who Arys quite desperately needed was the first woman who didn't try to practically strip herself naked...well, she was nearly that already. So many women through that Gate, and this one, *this one*, Cray wanted. And she did not want him. Did not want to want him.

Which meant he would not be having her.

And Arys kept staring at him with blank eyes as though he feared the pretty little witch was going to change her mind and throw herself into Cray the Fallen's arms and they would fly away.

How many women had come through the Gate? Dozens, easily. And quite a few had been attracted to Arys. At first. But Daklin would arrive. Or another elf. Or Cray. Rarely Ronal. From time to time one of the other Guardians would come to escort Arys' refugees to a place of sanctuary. And the woman would leave, practically wrapping her legs around the newcomer's waist, and not even glancing back at Arys, though often times, Cray suspected that was because Arys did everything to shove them out of the Satyr's Wood.

Bleeding Wing, the Satyr had seduced women away from the vampire, only to walk away when he desired the freedom of his wood. He had sunk his cock into elfin ladies and faerie princesses, yet he still let mortal after mortal walk away.

Of course, the angel suspected this was the first mortal that truly mattered.

Cray had wished Arys would stop calling out the other Guardians and just take the bloody females to their selected sanctuary on his own.

He was strong enough to be away from his wood for a few weeks.

Even months.

His magick was earth-grounded, but Arys wasn't exactly the average satyr.

Yes, provisions were made because he was the first satyr ever to be a Guardian. Most Guardians escorted or provided escort for the refugees themselves. But the satyr was a free spirit, had no servant or underlings and satyrs rarely left their woods—they *needed* the wood they were bound to. The Council had known provisions would be made, would have to be made for Arys.

But Arys was the only acceptable Guardian for this Gate.

The Gate had made that clear.

Of course, Cray suspected Arys hadn't let on just how well he was able to do away from his wood, or for how long. He simply didn't want to leave it.

He was tempted to sulk. But somehow he didn't think it was fitting that a man nearly eight centuries old be caught pouting.

Daklin caught his gaze.

And the elf winked.

Cray couldn't stop the snarl or the warning growl.

Daklin was still rubbing his burning hand. There were no marks there. The pain had been illusory. But he imagined she could have made it real. The pretty little witch had retreated behind a silk screen to clothe herself— *pity*—and was now sitting curled up beside Arys eating a piece of *beiori* fruit, an elvish fruit he had brought with him for Arys. She was still watching them with wide, suspicious eyes. Mismatched eyes, at that.

Cray was sprawled on the bed, brooding. *Poor fellow.* Daklin had seen the interest light the angel's silvery eyes the moment they had stepped clear of the portal. It had only intensified when Pepper hadn't shown him the normal jaw-dropping, eyes-glazing, lust-induced trance-like state so many mortal females went into.

"Not for us, Cray," he said silently, only for the angel.

"I am fully aware, you pointy-eared bastard. I've several centuries on you, not to mention being smarter than a bloody elf even on my worst day, boy," Cray replied.

Daklin laughed, his head falling back, sending his blond hair falling behind the chair, almost to the floor. At nearly six-hundred-years-old, not many people referred to Daklin as *boy*. Cray could get by with it, because he was Cray. *"Stop acting like a snow bear who got his paw caught in a hunter's trap. It is not very polite."*

"Fuck off." But Cray's wings ruffled and shook as he stood up and tossed his hair out of his face. He couldn't stand the thought of a lovely woman, one he was attracted to, thinking he was sulking.

Once Cray was settled at the high, backless well-padded stool Arys had made especially for him, Daklin paused to smile and say to Pepper, "My Gate opens to India, France, and Spain. Those tongues, I know quite well. English only little. And what I must bespeak is both urgent and important. The satyr can explain later. And will, I know. Your forgiveness I beg for this impropriety."

Pepper arched a red brow at him, the one over her blue eye as she said, "You speak so very prettily for somebody who doesn't understand my language very well."

Cray grinned.

Arys sighed as his head fell back against the padded lounge where he and Pepper cuddled together. His eyes closed and he looked to be praying for patience. But Daklin could see the amusement on his face, the happiness. He hoped the news he was bringing didn't kill that.

Daklin narrowed his eyes and just studied the sassy little witch. "Well-matched you are," he murmured, shaking his head. "Very well, indeed."

Falling back into Mitaro, a blend of elvish, human, and trader's tongue, Daklin rapidly said, "You must come to Asquiro. The Summit must be held. The Watchers will watch the Gate. It is quiet now, yes? We have problems. Watchers going missing. Gatekeepers going missing. Sorcerers and witches in training missing from their beds. Ronal had to destroy one of the lesser Gates in his territory."

Arys frowned, his face going grim. "How long has this been going on?"

"We know not for certain," Cray said, his voice softer, slower in Mitaro. He gave Daklin a grim glance. "A year at least. Possibly two. The sister of one of the missing witches came to the Council to alert us, but was turned away. She then came to me, but that was only two months ago. She did some inquiring of her own before she told anybody. Her inquiry took three months, and it shed more light. Three other witches, one male. Two female. Two sorcerers. Both male. Both known for being...tricky sorts."

"By the Blood," Arys murmured, shaking his head. He closed his hands into fists, feeling the sharp bite of his nails into his palms. Sorcerers, damn the lot of them. Unlike witches, sorcerers used blood to finish their magicks and it was all too easy for them to follow a darker path. "And the Gatekeepers?"

"Young ones, all. Three of them. A faerie, a breed-vamp, and a mortal with a knack for earth magick. All females." Cray's eyes darkened to the color of thunderheads and the air in the *iskita* grew heavy and thick, as though a storm were ready to burst. "None of their superiors have been able to reach them. None of them have been heard from in nearly three months time."

"And this is the first I have heard," Arys said darkly, rising slowly. "Am I lesser than you?"

"No." Daklin's eyes narrowed, the blue darkening to near sapphire in his anger, his cheeks flushing in his own rage. "Apparently the Council just now decided the rest of us needed to be informed. Cray went to them and was led to believe we were all informed. He was unable to stay, or come to me and tell me himself, because he had problems at his keep. I was having problems in the realm. *Problems.* They are arising all over the bloody world, it would seem."

"Ronal is the reason we all now know," Cray said quietly. "The breed-vamp is one of his offspring. He sired her birth mother. And her birth mother went to visit her and went into panic when she couldn't find her. She and her human mate went to Ronal and Ronal, being the noble bastard he is, went searching for her. There was...*something* he called it, *something dark and deadly like nothing I have ever felt in all my years.*"

Arys felt a cold shiver run down his spine. His lashes drooped to hide his expression and he blanked his face. Cold and sudden horror filled him. Ronal was even older than Cray. He had seen his first millennium. He had outlived even the Gatekeeper who had originally lived in the wood before Arys had taken over care of the Gate. Damis had died in a freak accident nearly a century ago and the mortal sorcerer had been 959 years old. Rumor had it that he had barely looked a day over fifty.

"He did not bother going to the Council. He activated the mirror and told every Gatekeeper he could find. That was three days ago. You must not have been...available.

Then he deigned to advise the Council. The Council, of course, was a bit...upset," Daklin said, a smile dancing around his mouth. But the Council was not very likely to reprimand a vampire, especially Ronal.

They were bloody terrified of him.

"That was when they decided to inform us of what all has been going on. They've known. All along, they have known. Something, someone is out there trying to pick us off one by one, and they have not bothered to warn us."

Chapter Six

Arys explained to Pepper while he was packing up what little he would take. "My friends will watch over you. There is plenty of food to last you, for weeks even. Faryn can help you find more, should you need —"

"Like hell," Pepper said calmly, reaching around him, plucking a pair of pants from the meager pile and pulling them up her legs. They were too snug around her hips and butt, she thought with a grimace, but it was better than being bare-assed. "I'm not staying in a strange place, where witches and sorcerers are going missing. And Gatekeepers, which is what *you* are.

"It is not safe outside my wood. The wood is far safer than the outside world. The magick beasts and creatures here are my friends and they will guard you with their lives. No harm will befall you, swear it, I will," Arys murmured, catching her hands and bringing her close, stroking her hair.

Her eyes narrowed, and she glared at him. "I'm not helpless." Pulling her hands away from him, she backed up a step and then another. "I'm not staying here alone."

"Not alone, my friends —"

Pepper closed her eyes, prayed for patience. Closing her hand around the cross at her throat, she took a deep breath before she opened her eyes and focused them on the man before her. "Let me put it this way. I'm not staying *here.* I'm coming with you. Period. End of discussion."

His eyes narrowed in confusion, head cocked, as he tried to figure out her wording. But he got the meaning and simply shook his head. "*Non.* Do not argue. I can force you to stay. The wood is mine, it will obey my orders. And Daklin is a magick worker as well as you. Shall he prove it?"

"Let him try," she dared.

Arys sighed. Plowing his hand through his hair, he stared at her. "Woman, you are stubborn. This is no pleasure trip I go on. We must travel hard. From your easy world, with your automobiles? We do not travel so. If it is decided that there is a warmonger among us, then one of us, or more, will be sent to stop him. Pretty rainbows and lights—no good will they be to us."

Her eyes widened then narrowed, and her mouth parted in a gasp. She flicked her hand toward him as indignation and rage coursed through her. She had never, *ever,* in her life had her skill questioned. Pretty rainbows and lights…is that what he thought she had?

Wind elements coursed from her to him and before Arys could even realize he might have made a small mistake, he was pinned by air against the wall of his *iskita.* "Pretty rainbows? Lights? Is that all?" she asked, arching a brow as the door opened. Wild, angry magick was a palpable thing and it was no surprise the elf and Cray had felt it.

Daklin took one look at Arys and opened his mouth, lifting a long-fingered, elegant hand. She felt the swell of power as he started to speak.

"Silence," she hissed, pointing at him. "Join him."

"Fuck," Daklin gasped as a fist of unseen power grabbed him and propelled him to the wall next to the satyr.

"What about you?"

Cray lifted a black brow. "I have no qualms if you care to join us, lady witch. I know a warrior witch well enough," he said slowly, bowing his head and backing out of the room, closing the door. His eyes were dancing with amusement all the while.

"I care not to battle a woman. Release me before I am angered enough to try," Daklin said quietly, clenching his fists. He wasn't certain, though, if he *could*. And that really angered him. There was an odd feel to her magick, one that was unlike elvish magick, unlike the witch's magick he knew, and the little minx knew it. By the Blood, she knew it.

"You should have minded your own business," she said archly, flopping down on the bed. She rolled onto her side, the lace of the neckline falling down to reveal the mound of one breast, molding to the dip of her waist, the rise of her hip under the tight fitting breeches she had appropriated from Arys. "This didn't concern you at all, Legolas."

"My name is Daklin, lady-witch," he growled.

"I know damn good and well what your name is, slick," she replied. She then proceeded to ignore him and propped her head on her hand, her red curls falling to the bed as she studied her silent lover.

"Still think I can't take care of myself, sugar?" she drawled, batting her lashes at Arys who was staring at her with dark, unreadable eyes. "Would you like to see what else I can do besides pretty lights and rainbows?"

When he only stared at her, she narrowed her eyes and whispered, "Fire." Then naughtily, "Fire, fire burning bright…"as flames burst merrily to life, inches above the floor, hot, searing hot, enough to have the men sweating inside a minute.

"Nice illusion," Daklin said in a bored tone.

She smiled coldly. "Touch it," she offered, releasing the elf only. He landed abruptly, only his catlike reflexes keeping him from a fall on his very nice ass. "Illusion after all won't harm you."

He arrogantly took her dare, passing his hand through and bellowing out a foreign curse as his shirt caught fire. She dampened the fire before it took hold enough to damage anything and rose to her feet, reached through the flames and jerked him through, the flames parting around her and not touching her flesh at all.

"Illusion?" she purred as she traced her hand over the second-degree burn already forming. She stared at him through a thick veil of lashes as she ran her fingers roughly over the blisters, while he stared at her wide-eyed.

"Fire to call so easily, no witch of Mythe has this. Nor the ability to reach through it without taking so much as a burn to her lovely flesh," he said roughly. "Simple is it, creating illusion. Creation of true fire, simply with the word, is something else, altogether."

She closed her hands over the burns on his hand and squeezed tightly, closing her eyes, not releasing as he hissed and tried to jerk his hand away. "Bloody hurts, you mean little—"then his voice trailed away as heat spread from her hands to his flesh. His jaw clenched, his eyes closed, his lids drooped as sweat formed on his brow.

She had to admire his restraint. It had to hurt, the healing of such a painful little burn. Second-degree burns, even small ones, were a bitch, and healing always took heat. Heat on a burn...not a nice feeling. But she sent a cool kiss of illusion as she pulled her hands away.

"A healer, as well," he whispered, cocking a brow at her while Arys continued to stare at them, the heat of anger in his eyes making the fire still burning at his feet look paltry.

The satyr was still unable to do more than blink or talk. Not that he had said even a word, though the fire burned only inches away from him.

"Only very little. I can do this, because I caused it," she said, lifting one shoulder. She slid her eyes to the door, and lifted her brows questioningly.

He bent slightly at the waist. "My most sincere apologies, lady witch. What I was thinking, I know not," he murmured, shaking his head. He cast Arys a long, meaningful glance through the merrily burning flames and left silently, closing the door behind him.

She doused the fire and studied the room. Not a singe mark in sight. "Wanna watch me pull a rabbit out of my hat?" she asked, her voice brittle, her eyes hard. She crossed the room and stood only inches away, as close to him as the flames had been. "I just found you. And I've been waiting for you all my life. I'm not letting you just leave me behind."

"This is no pleasure walk I take," he growled, flexing his muscles. He tossed his head back, his ebony hair whipping around his horns, his eyes gleaming slightly red with his rage, making him look a bit demonic. "Release me, damn it all. Months I may be gone. I know not. Think I would risk you?"

"Think I would risk *you?*" she snarled. "I'm a bloody witch! I'm not a young one either, or a weak one, or a foolish one. I'm not naive, and I'm not eager for more power. All I'm eager for is to be *with you.*" She let him down, hurled herself at him, fisted her hands in his hair and crushed her mouth brutally to his. His arms locked around her and he whirled her around, pinning her against the wall with a ragged groan. Tearing her mouth away, she gasped, "Try to make me stay, I dare you. I'd bet anything I can use that gate to follow you."

Arys' eyes closed and he slumped against her, shaking his head. "I imagine, yes, you could. Pepper, love, understand me, if something happens to you of all people, it will break me. My other half, you feel like," he murmured, threading his hands through her hair.

"Then you should understand why I can't let you leave me," she whispered.

"I imagine she will be joining us," Cray murmured as he paced outside in the small clearing, opening his wings, fanning them in the dappled sunlight.

"Bloody hell, she will. Arys is fucking enraged," Daklin said, shaking his head. He had threaded a series of sparkling beads through the set of braids on either side of his head and they made a small clacking sound as he shook his head. He still couldn't believe she had pinned him against the wall. Wind. Fire. Two elements. She had control of two elements. Complete control, not just a minor gift, but complete control. The witches of Mythe maybe could call one, and in time, those few could learn to control that element.

That young mortal already controlled *two*.

Cray laughed, a rare sound for the fallen one. "She bested you, elf, didn't she? Never imagined she'd have elemental magicks, did you? Illusions, herb magicks, maybe even a mind magicker or an enchanter like yourself…some sight…perhaps? But not elemental."

Daklin scowled at him, his sooty, gold-tipped lashes dropping down over his blue eyes as he made an obscene gesture at the angel and silkily said, "Would you like the ice maidens of the North to come calling on you, Cray?"

Cray only smiled.

Chapter Seven

They heard the door open and turned to see Arys standing there, his hands resting on Pepper's shoulders. "My lady will come," he said softly, firmly. "A wildling horse of Faryn's get will come for her to ride so that travel swiftly we may."

Daklin swore in elvish. In Mitaro, he said, "Arys, show some bloody sense. She knows nothing of our world. If we fall upon danger how can she protect herself? We will protect her with our lives, but what if something happens to *us*? She is safe here in the wood."

"I am not leaving her," Arys said softly in the same tongue, shaking his head. "She is right. I cannot. And she proved good and well that she is not helpless."

"But can she use it to *fight? Protect?* Damn it, you fool, think with your head, not your heart," Daklin insisted.

Cray moved closer, saying, "Daklin, the little witch is fully capable of taking care of herself. Like a little mountain cat, she is. She is like a warrior witch of old, I tell you. She will be fine."

"Cray, you've grown fanciful in your old age," Daklin scoffed, tossing his long blond locks over his shoulder, crossing his arms over his chest, muscles bulging. The small knife at his bicep winked in the light as he glared at both men, ignoring Pepper completely. "This is insanity. And she's to travel on a wildling—"

None had noticed that Pepper had gone stiff and white.

Her back arched, her nostrils flared.

Her hands itched, her scalp felt tight. "Arys, something is wrong," she whispered. He wasn't listening. The air around her seemed to be drawing tighter and tighter.

In the tongue she didn't understand, Daklin continued, "A fucking wildling horse. She'll be begging to return after a half day. And you'll not be riding her at all, she will be so sore."

Arys narrowed his eyes and advanced on the elf, flexing his hands, the nails on his long hands suddenly resembling claws. "Watch that tongue, elf. Or shall I cut it out? That is my lady you speak so crudely of," he rasped, his black eyes gleaming red with anger.

"Then think of her," Daklin shouted, his voice making the air around them tremble like thunderclouds had just clashed together over head as he thrust a bare, leanly muscled arm at her. The beads in his hair clinked together musically as his voice dropped to a rough whisper that was no less intense for its quietness. "Leave her here. Where she will—"

The sky opened.

The men moved quickly.

But not quickly enough, as they tried to locate the danger they just now started to sense.

Pepper moved like the black lightning that flared down out of it. She placed herself in the center of the three men, hands wide overhead and closed her eyes as the shield formed while she prayed and worked.

All I've ever needed was myself…

And faith.

But now she prayed for strength as well, because what was streaking down at her was like nothing she had ever imagined before.

Falling to his knees, swearing, Daklin drew the knife at his bicep, but it was too damn late for an enchantment ward. Enchantment took time, and they had none. And the stinking, black, powerful bolt coming down at them was their death. He pricked his finger and made the first mark, just as it hit, and he pitched to his side, clutching his knife, and rolling to his feet.

Arys moved to stand behind Pepper, protectively, possessively, proudly, at her back, a tiny little smile on his lips as he lifted his face to the trees and called upon his own form of magick while the ground started to shudder and tremble beneath their feet.

Cray hadn't fallen—he stood with his powerful legs braced, staring at the witch with wide, rapt, unblinking eyes, wings held tight and close to his body. The area around them was untouched. The immediate area beyond it was blackened and scorched for several yards, including the front half of the *iskita*.

Then beyond that, nothing, everything was pristine.

And they were all four still alive, inside a precise circle around the little redheaded witch.

Arys stood behind Pepper, his eyes closed...*feeding.* He was feeding the power he drew from the wood into his witch, who was shielding them. "One more," she whispered. "I can feel him...he doesn't know about me...but he is sending one more to make sure he got all of you. He knew Cray and Daklin were standing close, that first bolt was for them. This last one is for Arys. He wants you all dead. The Four Pillars."

The Four Pillars...Ronal...

Over her shoulder, Daklin met Arys' eyes. Feeling Cray's eyes on him as well, he shrugged and said softly, "A warrior witch, eh?" He closed the space between them and made the two marks for protection, one on her left cheek, one on her right, while they waited for the power to build.

He lowered his head and brushed his lips against hers. "My apologies, lady-witch," he murmured as his own shield surged to life, centering on her, the power feeding her as well.

She smiled slowly. "Go away...you're too pretty. You make it hard to concentrate," she said. Then she leaned her head back against Arys and focused on the black morass starting to form overhead.

* * * * *

"Someone tried to assassinate us," Arys murmured as he moved around his *iskita* and gathered up what was salvageable. "We must check on Ronal."

"That old bastard will be fine," Daklin said, shaking his head. And hoping. But in his gut, he knew the vampire was well. Little could take a vampire off guard, and the vampire could take to the skies when in danger.

"We will check," Cray said. "And then we will meet. Somebody will pay for this...betrayal."

He heard a bell peal, followed by a more insistent trumpet. Then Ronal's deep voice. "Satyr, if you hear my voice, *answer* me. *Now.*" Never had the vampire sounded so...insistent.

Arys moved to the mirror, which was untouched, and stroked the foggy surface with his fingers. It cleared and he swore when he saw Ronal. The vampire was in a killing rage. His fangs had dropped, his face had no color and his green eyes were glowing as he paced back and forth. Several nasty cuts and bruises marred his physique, but they were slowly knitting back together even as Arys stared at him.

When he saw the satyr's face, some of the rage left him, and his wide, proud shoulders shuddered as he took a deep breath. "Thank the Father of us all," Ronal said, moving to the mirror and resting both hands on the surface of it.

Arys mirrored the gesture and studied the vampire as everybody gathered around behind him.

Ronal studied Pepper for a brief moment and then smiled at Arys, slowly, satisfied. Then he said, "I had an...incident. And a sickening fear that it had happened to you as well. And only Cray would be able to flee as fast as I. And Cray would never leave his brethren behind."

"An incident of our own," Arys said, moving to the side while the others parted, allowing Ronal to see the destroyed *iskita*. He absently stroked one of his horns while he wrapped his other arm around Pepper, drawing her close to his side. "It seems as though we have an enemy who was just waiting for a time when he had more than one of us together in one place."

Ronal swore, long and vicious, in his tongue, one fist striking the mirror. "I must ask, though I am grateful you survived. How did you? I watched, and if any but I had been in the chamber..."

Arys pushed Pepper in front of the mirror even though she resisted. "She is how. She felt it. Meet my lady, Ronal. She is called Pepper, and she is from the mortal realms. A warrior witch, Cray has called her. And well said, it would seem," he murmured, lowering his head to nuzzle her neck. Wrapping his arms tightly around her, he continued, "Felt the dark magick coming, did my lady. *Oui*, she felt it, she shielded us, saved us. A warrior witch. Pretty, pretty mine."

Pepper blushed as he crooned against her neck, while the newcomer studied her with appraising eyes. *Warrior witch*. It gave her an odd little thrill to be called that. Of course, the thrill could be coming from him pressing his hot mouth to her neck while three other men watched with curious eyes.

"I believe your lady is embarrassed, Arys," Ronal said with a smile. A long, slow shudder racked his body and as she watched, the fangs protruding past his lips withdrew slightly and some color reappeared on his face. "It is a good thing that I see my friends alive and unharmed. A good thing."

"We must meet," Cray said.

"Aye," Ronal murmured, turning his gaze back to Pepper, his moss green eyes dark with curiosity. "That we must." He spoke English. Very well, in fact. Better, it seemed, than Arys. "But we will need a safer haven than what I know. I would suggest —"

"My people's realm," Daklin said, stepping forward, lifting a brow.

Ronal sneered at the elf. "Ever the do-gooder, aren't you, long ear? But…that is exactly what I was going to suggest, you lovely thing," he said drolly. "But I have a fear that a vampire would not be welcome in the fair kingdom of the elves."

Daklin coolly replied, "If you can keep your sharp teeth away from our virgin women, you are welcome."

Ronal smiled. "I prefer my women with more years on them anyway. Got any sisters, Daklin?"

Pepper whispered to Arys, "I thought they were friends."

"They are," he responded. "Elves and vampires...do not exactly make easy friends. Like fire and ice they are."

Cray laughed. "More like heaven and hell," he offered. "And take your pick, lady witch, of who is the angel or demon." He nodded his head toward the dark-haired vampire and the fair-haired elf who snapped back and forth through the mirror.

It was in a small cabin that she spent her last night in Arys' wood.

Alone, with her satyr.

She stared at him nervously as he came through the doorway, uncertain how to take the odd gleam she saw in his eyes. *Is he still mad about the fire thing?*

Cray and Daklin had made themselves scarce. Where they had gone to sleep for the night she didn't know. Hadn't really cared at the time. And she didn't really think she cared now...but the odd light in Arys' eyes was making her nervous.

He closed the door behind him and studied the small cabin. "Not the *iskita*, but it shall suffice," he murmured, sliding her a sidelong glance as he removed the pack at his back and shucked his breeches.

He was nude when he faced her.

Pepper stared at him hungrily, curling her fingers into tight fists as she dragged her eyes up his long lean form. *So damn exotic, so handsome...* Her mouth had gone dry, her nipples were tight and erect and her sex was wet and aching, just from staring at him.

"Too many clothes, pretty witch," he said as he closed the distance between them.

Awkwardly she tugged the shirt over her head, gasping as she felt his hot mouth close over the hard tip of one nipple as his hands went to the waist of her trousers and jerked them down. "Mine," he purred against her skin. "Say it."

"Yours," she whispered raggedly as he plunged two fingers inside her pussy, twisting his wrist back and forth as he worked his fingers in and out. "And you're mine."

"Yours," he agreed, crowding against her and pushing her down onto the bed, pushing her thighs apart and leaning in, drawing his wicked tongue up her wet slit, humming in appreciation before stiffening his tongue and thrusting it deep inside, over and over, until she was rocking up against his mouth and whimpering.

"Tasty, sweet," he crooned against her, moving up and flicking his tongue against her clit, pushing his fingers back inside her and listening to her scream as she tightened around them and wailed. The silken walls of her vagina clenched down, spasmodically, rhythmically, and as he pushed inside a second, then a third time, she started to come, rocking up against his hand and mouth and pleading in a broken little voice, "Again, oh, please...there, right there, please...Arys...*Arys!*"

He covered her quickly and drove deep inside, working past the tightening of her muscles as she came, shuddering as her silken pussy gripped his cock so tightly. Catching her tossing head in his hands, he took her mouth roughly and plunged his tongue deep inside, groaning as she wrapped her legs around his waist and pulled him tightly against her, the heels of her feet digging in just above his ass.

He reached down and gripped her firmly muscled ass with one hand, digging his nails into her flesh and feeling her shocked, aroused little moan as he traced his finger against the opening of her rosette.

The diamond-hard points of her nipples stabbed into him and he shifted again, bending down and catching one of the rosy, plump tips in his mouth, biting down and suckling strongly as he pushed his cock deep inside her sweet, wet depths. She shrieked and tightened around him, starting to climax again, just as the last one faded, the scream falling, ragged and weak, from her lips.

Chuckling, he brushed a kiss against her trembling lips and whispered, "Slow down." Then he shifted onto his knees, draping her thighs over his, spreading her open, staring down where his cock entered her. Arys watched as the tender pink flesh of her pussy stretched tightly around his dark, ruddy cock. The sweet, slick cream from her orgasm made his cock gleam as he pulled out slowly and surged back inside. Sliding his hands under her ribcage, arching her back up, he swiveled his hips and drove his shaft high inside her.

The satin-slicked, swollen tissues tensed around him and she shuddered, sobbing as her hands fisted in the linens beneath her, her eyes glassy and blind. "Arys…"

"Sweet, hot little mine," he crooned, bringing one hand around and stroking the flat of his palm down her torso, resting the heel of his hand on her pubis and circling his thumb over the swollen bud of her clit.

Each time she started to tense and tighten as she neared orgasm, his hand retreated—stroking her ass, tweaking her nipple—until she was crying and pleading.

Slicked with sweat, her lips swollen and bruised, she sobbed, "Arys, please, I need you."

Lost, needing her so desperately, he released his control, hunkering over her and shafting her with strong, deep strokes. His cock burrowed deep, retreating and then filling her again as he fucked her roughly, his long, lean body shuddering as he rose up and gripped her hips. Driving deep, staring down at where they joined, he watched as he pushed his cock inside the snug embrace of her sex. Watched the feathery curls of her mound tangle with the fine pelt that covered his lower body, and the way her cream had the smooth skin of his cock gleaming and ruddy as he slammed back into her.

"Bloody hell," he swore as his balls drew tight and he exploded into her just as she thrust her hips up and ground her pelvis against him. She locked her hands around his wrists and worked herself against him, her teeth setting into the plump curve of her lip as she sobbed out his name.

The milking sensations from her pussy emptied him and he slumped forward, catching his weight on his hands and rolling to his side, taking her with him and cuddling her against him, murmuring against her brow, "Love you, mine…pretty, pretty mine…"

She wriggled against him and wrapped an arm around his neck, kissing the damp skin she found there and sighing with bliss. And against his neck, she purred, "Love you, my satyr."

Enjoy this excerpt from

VOYUER

© Copyright Shiloh Walker 2003

Voyeur

"…a strong plot...beautifully written to delight any reader…a stirring story of love lost and love found with a slight twist." ~*Patricia McGrew, Sensual Romance*

Make sure you have some kleneex nearby. First to wipe the sweat from your forehead. Then to wipe the tears from your eyes. This story has it all- tears, laughter, love and mind-blowing sex. ~*Jenni, A Romance Review*

"…one of the most beautifully written love stories I've ever read…two breathtakingly beautiful love stories…a thought provoking work of literature…If you want raw sex so hot it's hard to breathe, read this book." ~*Maggie O. The Romance Studio*

Chapter One

"Who would you like to ride while I screw your ass?"

Ashlyn stiffened, and buried her face in the pillow. They had moved to the bed after cleaning up and she had been drifting off to sleep.

It wasn't an unusual question, at least not from Kye. He seemed determined to share her with somebody, determined to slide inside her ass with tiny, invading thrusts while somebody else lay beneath her, fucking her in a more traditional manner.

As thrilling as the idea seemed, she wasn't about to let it happen. She knew herself too damn well and suspected if the time for such a treat ever came, she'd probably run scared. Ashlyn was not the adventurous type, or at least, she didn't think she was.

Anal sex was certainly something she had never considered. Kye had practically begged, and she still hadn't given in. It had taken him months to talk her into.

And hell, the first time she had let Kye give it to her in the ass, she had been more than a little tipsy. And the second time. "But by the third, and fourth times...she had come to crave it.

But another man in the bed? Not likely. She'd feel like a deer in the headlights — caught, fascinated — and then she'd turn into a rabbit and run like hell.

"Lay off it, Kye," she muttered, wanting to fall into the waiting maw of oblivion. With the exception of the past hour, the whole day had sucked. And tomorrow was going to be just as bad. The pediatric office where she worked had turned into hell on earth. Temporarily. One nurse on maternity leave. Another sick. And everybody just *had* to get in that day. Or the next. But only after four o'clock.

She snuggled into her pillow and yawned, the demands of the past few days catching up with her.

"Come on," he cajoled, fondling her breast as he propped himself on his elbow.

"Kye, it won't happen. "With a sigh, she pushed up until she sat, and drew her knees to her chest. "Maybe I do want to try it, once. But I'm neurotic enough that it will have to be somebody we know, somebody we can trust. And I'd like it to be somebody I don't personally know. An anonymous stranger I know we can trust, how likely is that? It would also have to be somebody I'll never have to see again. I'd probably die from embarrassment. Facts, disturbing, distressing, embarrassing facts that I just can't get past, but hey, that's life."

Tugging her down next to him, he considered that while he rubbed her back. "Go to sleep," he murmured.

About the author:

Shiloh was born in Kentucky and has been reading avidly since she was six. At twelve, she discovered how much fun it was to write when she took a book that didn't end the way she had wanted it to and rewrote the ending. She's been writing ever since.

Shiloh now lives in southern Indiana with her husband and two children. Between her job, her two adorable and demanding children, and equally adorable and demanding husband, she crams writing in between studying and reading and sleeps when time allows.

Shiloh welcomes mail from readers. You can write to her c/o Ellora's Cave Publishing at 1337 Commerce Drive, Suite 13, Stow OH 44224.

Also by Shiloh Walker:

Coming In Last
Firewalkers: Dreamer
Her Best Friend's Lover
Her Wildest Dreams
Hot Spell
Make Me Believe
Once Upon A Midnight Blue
The Dragon's Warrior
The Hunters: Byron and Kit
The Hunters: Delcan and Tori
The Hunters: Eli and Sarel
The Hunters: Jonathan and Lori
Touch of Gypsy Fire
Voyeur
Whipped Cream and Handcuffs

Why an electronic book?

We live in the Information Age—an exciting time in the history of human civilization in which technology rules supreme and continues to progress in leaps and bounds every minute of every hour of every day. For a multitude of reasons, more and more avid literary fans are opting to purchase e-books instead of paperbacks. The question to those not yet initiated to the world of electronic reading is simply: *why?*

1. *Price.* An electronic title at Ellora's Cave Publishing runs anywhere from 40-75% less than the cover price of the <u>exact same title</u> in paperback format. Why? Cold mathematics. It is less expensive to publish an e-book than it is to publish a paperback, so the savings are passed along to the consumer.

2. *Space.* Running out of room to house your paperback books? That is one worry you will never have with electronic novels. For a low one-time cost, you can purchase a handheld computer designed specifically for e-reading purposes. Many e-readers are larger than the average handheld, giving you plenty of screen room. Better yet, hundreds of titles can be stored within your new library—a single microchip. (Please note that Ellora's Cave does not endorse any specific brands. You can check our website at www.ellorascave.com for customer

recommendations we make available to new consumers.)

3. *Mobility.* Because your new library now consists of only a microchip, your entire cache of books can be taken with you wherever you go.

4. *Personal preferences are accounted for.* Are the words you are currently reading too small? Too large? Too...**ANNOYING**? Paperback books cannot be modified according to personal preferences, but e-books can.

5. *Innovation.* The way you read a book is not the only advancement the Information Age has gifted the literary community with. There is also the factor of what you can read. Ellora's Cave Publishing will be introducing a new line of interactive titles that are available in e-book format only.

6. *Instant gratification.* Is it the middle of the night and all the bookstores are closed? Are you tired of waiting days—sometimes weeks—for online and offline bookstores to ship the novels you bought? Ellora's Cave Publishing sells instantaneous downloads 24 hours a day, 7 days a week, 365 days a year. Our e-book delivery system is 100% automated, meaning your order is filled as soon as you pay for it.

Those are a few of the top reasons why electronic novels are displacing paperbacks for many an avid reader. As always, Ellora's Cave Publishing welcomes your questions and comments. We invite you to email us at service@ellorascave.com or write to us directly at: 1337 Commerce Drive, Suite 13, Stow OH 44224.

Discover for yourself why readers can't get enough of the multiple award-winning publisher Ellora's Cave. Whether you prefer e-books or paperbacks, be sure to visit EC on the web at www.ellorascave.com for an erotic reading experience that will leave you breathless.

Printed in the United States
29810LVS00004B/61-540